GRACE'S DAY

WILLIAM WALL is the author of four
previous novels, three volumes of short
stories and four collections of poetry. His
work has won many awards, including the
Virginia Faulkner Award and the 2017
Drue Heinz Literature Prize. His 2005
novel, *This is the Country*, was longlisted
for the Man Booker Prize.

Also by William Wall

Novels

Alice Falling
Minding Children
The Map of Tenderness
This is the Country

Short Stories

No Paradiso
Hearing Voices Seeing Things
The Islands

Poetry

Mathematics And Other Poems
Fahrenheit Says Nothing To Me
Ghost Estate
The Yellow House

GRACE'S DAY

William Wall

NEW ISLAND   An Apollo Book

First published by New Island Books in 2018

This Apollo book first published in the UK by Head of Zeus in 2018
This paperback edition published in the UK in 2019
by Head of Zeus Ltd

9 7 5 3 1 2 4 6 8

A catalogue record for this book is available from the British Library.

ISBN (PB): 9781788545488
ISBN (E): 9781788545464

Typeset by JVR Creative India

Printed and bound by CPI Group (UK) Ltd,
Croydon, CR0 4YY

Head of Zeus Ltd
First Floor East
5–8 Hardwick Street
London EC1R 4RG
WWW.HEADOFZEUS.COM

For Liz

'In nature nothing exists alone.'

Rachel Carson, *Silent Spring*

Part One

One

A long time ago I had two sisters and we lived on an island. There was me and Jeannie and Em. They called me Grace, but I have never had much of that. I was an awkward child. I still am all these years later. Our house had two doors, one to the south, one to the north. Its garden looked towards the setting sun. It was a garden of apple trees and fuchsia and everything in it leaned away from the wind. Dry stone walls encircled it and sheep and children broke them down. My mother lived there with us. Boats came and went bringing food and sometimes sheep, and there were times when we lived by catching fish and rabbits, though we were not so good at either. Richard Wood came in the *Iliad*, his wooden yawl, always it seemed when a gale of wind was threatened. He dropped his anchor in the sound and stayed for nights at a time. Mother said he liked his home comforts. He was younger than her, though not by much, and she was younger than father. Father liked to come first, she said. In summer time we swam naked in the crystal water and saw his anchor bedded in the sand, the marks the chain left where it swung to tide or wind. Many a time I swam down that chain, hauling myself deeper hand over hand until I could stand on the bottom. But Richard took no notice. In calm weather we could see my footprints on the seabed as if I lived down there and had stood a long time in one place looking up. Or perhaps that was not how it happened. Words have that way of invading memory, the stories they tell us become our stories. What I remember and what I forget may be one and the same thing, or they may merely depend upon each other. And what my father remembered for me.

There were three islands and they were youth, childhood and age, and I searched for my father in every one.

Two

My first memory, the first memory that I can certainly say wasn't given me by someone else is of my father hoisting me onto his shoulders so that I could see something. What do you see Jeannie, he says, what do you see? We're in a crowd and my mother Jane is there. I don't remember whether my sister Grace is there or not and I don't know what it is that I want to see. It must have been before Em was born. What I remember most clearly is the enormous sense of safety and sureness coupled with a giddy vertigo. I remember looking down on the crowd. Many men wear cloth caps and the women wear scarves, as they did still in those days, and my father is smoking a pipe and I can smell the tobacco. One man turns and says something like, What you think of that then Tom? And Tom takes the pipe from his mouth, releasing my leg in the process, and says something I don't catch. Even now it only needs someone to light a pipe outside a restaurant for a great wave of security to possess me. Tom was not a tall man but from the height of his shoulders everyone around looked small. Hold on Jeannie, he said to me, and swung round and moved through the crowd and out onto the street and there I see a horse, a man is holding him by the bridle, and I remember steam coming off his back and steam coming from a large greenish-brown shit on the road behind him. I can smell the horse and he smells like Tom's old coat.

All my early memories of him are like that. Shelter, comfort, pleasant smells and sounds. I hear his voice sometimes – in the street or in a park or in a quiet room – and I turn expecting to see him. My expectation is always of a young man, trim, loose limbed, fine boned, coming towards me in his tweed jacket with something in his hand. My father the gift-bringer, bearer of news, the world traveller bringing stones from Italy, California, India. I was a collector of stones. I was his favourite. I make no apologies. I loved him the most. Grace, on the other hand, could never love anyone or anything without some reserve of herself; she has a kind of native hostility or cynicism that prevents her from ever being wholeheartedly loving towards anybody. She's one of those people who feels the world has cheated her of some special experience. I pity her for that.

Three

One day on our island my sister Jeannie ran in to say that she had seen a whale in the sound and I ran out after her, my mother calling me: Grace, it's your day, take Em. But I was too excited. And there were three fin whales making their way into the rising tide. We heard their breathing. It carried perfectly in the still grey air, reflected back at us by the low cloud. The sea was still and burnished. We ran along the rocks watching for their breaching. We decided it was a mother, a father and a calf. They were in no hurry. When we reached the beacon, a small unlit concrete marker indicating the western end of the island, we watched them breaching and diving into the distance until we could see them no more. But they left behind their calmness and the unhurried but forceful sound of their blows. We were wearing our summer shorts, and so, once the whales were no longer to be seen, I pulled mine off, threw Jeannie my shirt and plunged in and swam out into the rising tide and allowed myself to be carried along outside everything and back to the anchorage. That was how, so far out, drifting like a seal in the tide, I saw my mother kissing Richard Wood against the gable of our house. It did not come as a shock or a surprise but I felt a sickening sense of guilt and shame and I allowed myself to be carried past the anchored yawl and too far out into the sound, so that it was a struggle and a hard swim to get back. My sisters, Jeannie and Em, watched me sullenly for a long time. I think if I had drowned they would have watched that too with the same sullen disinterest. When I came ashore I was exhausted. I threw myself down on the strand and lay staring at the clouds for a long time. My mother was wearing her slacks and a jumper. Her sleeves were rolled back. She had put on weight and I could clearly see the bulge of her stomach low down, pressed against his belt. His hands were on her back inside the jumper. They could not have been seen from the shore. At that time my father was already in England. His name was mentioned in newspapers and from time to time when he wrote home, usually sending a cheque, he included clippings and reviews.

It's possible that Jeannie already hated me because while I lay on the sand she prised a large stone out of the shale and brought it steadfastly towards me, approaching from behind, and dropped it on my chest. The shock almost stopped my breath. I think she may well have been trying to kill me, but at five or six she simply didn't have the height to do it. The stone simply didn't reach a sufficient velocity. It landed flat and made a flat sound that I heard in my body rather than felt and I was too stunned to cry. I feel certain she dropped it on my chest rather than my head because she wanted to stop my heart. Had she been older she would have tried for my brain instead.

By the time I had recovered my breath she was gone. I searched for her, steadily and ruthlessly working my way west through the hiding places that I knew, and found her near the old tower, crouched in the bracken. She had already forgotten why she was hiding. She had feathers and a collection of bracken fronds, playing some game that involved talking in voices. She did not hear my approach. I caught her from behind by the hair, which was shoulder length at that time, and swung her onto her back. I was on her then and we fought hard, scratching and pulling and in the end we had each other by the hair, slapping and pinching and kicking until rolling off me she struck her head on a stone and began to cry. I can see her now, a pitiful, snotty-nosed waif curled in a ball, holding her head and wailing for her mother. Now I feel nothing but shame at the memory but at the time I laughed at her, because children know that laughing is the most hurtful reaction to pain, and she ran away again.

She was gone for the rest of the day and we had to search the island to bring her home for tea. By then the calm was gone and Richard Wood was talking anxiously about his anchor and declaring repeatedly that he should make a run for it, and my mother was pressing him to stay.

My father's books, and his colour pieces for the *Manchester Guardian*, depicting a family surviving on an island on the edge of the world, part fiction part memoir, were all the rage when we were children. This was the late 1960s and the world had fallen in love simultaneously with two incompatible mistresses – self-sufficiency and conspicuous consumption. The books represented the former, but my father, I would eventually discover, was more given at a personal level to the latter. It is my mother, my sisters and I who held the responsibility of acting out the life he felt bound to follow. We were the ones who lived in what he liked to call the peasant economy.

We called it Castle Island, but there never was a castle only a lonely watchtower, tall enough to survey the whole island and the sound and the ocean beyond, part of a network of revenue gathering outposts, not to mention occasional piracy some time in the fifteenth century, and now just two walls on the side of a cliff where even the crows did not think it safe to nest. He bought the land with the advance from his first book – in those days you couldn't give land away in Ireland – and installed us in what had been the last occupied house on the sheltered eastern shore, near a sweet well, a sheltered anchorage, in the shadow of the apple orchard, a small sandy strand. We were his experiment, he took readings of us as required. We were his instruments and his Utopia.

There were fields where we tried to grow potatoes and salt-burnt kale and onions. Other things too perhaps that I have not remembered. We kept hens one summer and had eggs for breakfast dinner and tea until the time came to pack up and leave again. Then there was nothing we could do for the hens. The following spring there was no trace of them. We never repeated the experiment. We had a cat who kept the mice at bay – Flanagan was his name. He was white as snow and his eyes were like stones. When father was there he set a fixed trotline of hooks across the mouth of the strand and in the morning he often had fish – plaice, dabs, flounder, bass. Our job was to dig the worms at low tide and hunt under rocks for ragworm, and in the evenings to thread the hooks with the worms and lay them out in a special way. He took photographs. *The children baiting hooks*. We appear in more than one volume. In the morning he pulled the silver creatures ashore and we cooked plaice for breakfast and had bass for dinner. This was before the fishery had been ruined. He wrote about it all, of course: *Living An Island, Loving the World*, by Tom Newman. Now out of print.

When he was at home the house was warmer, fuller, brighter; it functioned as a home and a house, and we functioned as a family. When he went away we settled back into our animal existence. After a few weeks without him the house lost his presence. It began to be possible to think of him as a character we had read about, someone of enormous energy and vision whose part had been to bring life to the other characters, a catalyst at work among lethargic elements. But the elements only appeared lethargic. Things happened that no one has ever explained. And the dynamic by which we related was frightening and selfish and destructive. When I think of it now I realise that it was not that he made things happen, but that he prevented things from happening. And when he was away there was no god to stand in the doorway and watch inside and out, and what happened inside the house and what happened in the fields, in the orchard and along the shore were both separate and different, and inseparable and the same.

Richard Wood was a poet and my father's friend, but he was of course also my mother's and my sister Jeannie's lover. He was a beautiful man. He was tall and thin and he moved his limbs with the grace of one who was at home in several elements. We thought he understood the air and could tell from simply breathing it what tomorrow would bring. He understood the shapes of clouds and had categorised them and knew rhymes that interpreted them.

Mackerel skies and mares' tails, he would say, make lofty ships carry low sails.

Or: When the rain comes before the wind, topsail sheets and halyards mind.

It was a kind of knowledge that was useful on an island and we wanted it. I see him standing on the highest rock in the face of the marching seas and looking to windward like a god or a figure in a painting. I don't think he ever did that, but the memory is there, as real as a fact. Richard, what do you see? Is the future in the wind? Not now my dear, not now. More than once he said to me that what landsmen think of as the smell of the sea was, to a sailor, the smell of the land and the smell of danger.

He knew the meaning of the weather systems and could tell by the frequency and length of waves how far away a new gale might be. He understood the compass and the Admiralty chart with its discrete symbolism and fine lines. He could calculate tides and knew when his keel would scrape over the bar and when it would run into the sand. He knew the changes in the seabed from mile to mile, and he knew what places would be bad on a rising tide and westerly wind, and what would be bad on an ebb or with the wind in the east. He was, in a way, a more primitive man than my father. But he was also more elegant and refined. My father had been born a Catholic, whereas Richard had been born into the last vestiges of the ascendancy class. He spoke with that standard Anglo-Irish accent. He had been to a boarding school in England where he had learned to write poetry about poor people and to ignore anyone he didn't choose to notice.

He fell in love with my mother when he heard her reading aloud to my father in the residents' lounge of a hotel. This is the story my mother told me, although when it took place, and whether it was for my father she was reading, and what the hotel was I never knew. Something about the way she told it years later suggested that it was an invention.

He had been asleep in a chair facing the window and they thought they were alone. She had taken a copy of Shelley's works from the hotel's bookshelves and was mockingly declaiming 'The Masque Of Anarchy'. That was in the days when hotels kept a store of the classics in case their guests were at a loss for something to do; nowadays they buy their books from interior designers. He fell in love with her then, she said.

So, we grew up on an island which was, in memory and in fact, more like a film set of my father's devising than a real place. Even as we children lived it, it had a second-hand feel, a parallel untouchable reality that was more like the reality of art. But of that reality there is this to say:

It was less than half a mile long. It was shallow at its eastern end and the strange behaviour of tides left sand in the long interstices of the rocks. Even on calm days there was the rumour of sea among stones, the grinding of pebbles. Between ourselves and The Calf, which was the next island in the sound, was a channel of about half a mile, ten fathoms deep at its most profound, but also containing a bar of the same sand which dried to a sheet of lead at the lowest spring tides. Seabirds met there in gabbling congregation for the cockles and so did we, Jeannie and I. The cockles were delicious. Jeannie would crack them open on a stone and eat them raw. Mother boiled them in milk.

Long ago the land had been divided by dry-stone walls into fields of varying sizes. Now the couch grass was thick as a cushion everywhere, and wherever the limestone pavement came close to the surface heather had possession. The man from whom we bought our house still owned some of these fields and we let him graze ours. He brought sheep here in the spring and so we never owned a dog, although a dog might have been a friend, and might have warned us against trouble when it came.

On the height, on the cliff that faced towards the mainland, was the ruined watchtower, and in the shadow of the watchtower a cluster of ruined cottages. The ground among the cottages seemed to be always wet. There was a spring there, I think, anyway the sheep went there to drink. Under the tower was an ancient crumbling pier and slipway. There was an iron bollard and a rusted windlass. We could have recovered the windlass – it was one of my father's projects – the parts were all intact, and if we had recovered it we could have used the slip to haul our boat out of the way of the sea, but it was never done and instead we hauled it up on the sand at high water and carried the anchor up into the grass. Sometimes we swam here, but I was the only one who would jump from the pier. At high tide the drop was ten feet, but at the bottom of the ebb it was almost twenty-five. The water was deep in any case and I was always the fearless one. I belonged to the sea as much as the land. My mother said I was one of the sea people and the seals were my cousins. And I believed her. They loved my grey-green eyes and I loved their slow cool appraisal of everything. Whenever I saw one I wanted to take my clothes off and follow. I imagined an inverted life where the wave was my sky, an underwater world of the underside of boats and islands and the mountains of the continental shelf.

Gales came and went, of course, because our home was a tiny island in the face of the Atlantic. Seas came to us from other continents. A fetch of a thousand miles is nothing to a storm. There were nights when it seemed the universe was conspiring to drown us all, with the air and rain falling on our house it was as though we lived inside a tin drum. Later when daylight came we would look to see if apple trees had come down, if there was seaweed in the branches, blisters of salt spume, if the ditches were littered with things from the water. The sea boiled over the rocks consuming and retiring, consuming and retiring, bright green and white and iron-grey, the surface, as far as the grey uncertain horizon, fretted, broken, chaotic. Those were the days I loved.

But once I remember a yacht going by, water streaming over its leeward deck, hard-pressed in a sudden gale, and one of the crew had a long handline out; it was the mackerel season. But they had caught a seagull, or more likely the seagull caught the hook, as happens when the line is towed too fast and the lead hops from wave to wave. And they were towing the terrified bird about fifteen feet from the stern. Eventually they cut the line and the gull tried to fly with the trace and the lead, but he kept losing height and dropping back into the water. The weight of the lead was too much for him. In the end I couldn't watch. I went away and when I came back the bird was gone and the boat was gone. There was only the wind and the brutal sea.

My mother was a storyteller. She told us tales of the undersea, of people who had fallen in love with the big dark eyes of the seal and the smooth body, people who forgot that their element was air. They were lost to their families and friends, and even when, occasionally, someone found a sea-woman in a net and brought her home, the undersea was always drawing her back especially at the spring tides when the sea was full and round as a belly. She told us these things at night when everything is more important, and outside the sea snored among the caves and arches and the curlews called. She told the stories from one or other of our beds, with the blankets pulled up to her chin because her toes were always cold, taking each bed in turn. We three children always fought over whose bed was next. She would turn out the light, and sometimes there was moonlight and sometimes there was none. She began every story in the same way: My mother told me. So that we came to believe that only women knew these things. And perhaps we were right. And in addition, we thought that a story so ancient had to be true, at least in ancient times however changed the world was in ours. I remember the moonlight slanting in across the room, her low soft voice, Em's breathing. Sometimes Flanagan the cat was there, curled up on the end of the bed.

But one summer there was a fisherman and he would come and drink whiskey after he had set his pots. He was a tall handsome man. His face was dried and grained by the sea. His eyes had the wind in them, such a blue as you see on dry hard days. My mother welcomed the company and I think he wanted her, or wanted her presence. He never came when Richard's yawl was anchored in the bay. He had been ten years in the boats he said, in the fleets on the North Sea. The cod fisheries were dying. The Grand banks were empty. He told us of times when he had been sent aloft to chip ice from the mast lest they capsize with the weight of it. More than once I saw him catch my mother's hand. And she let him do it. She was like that. She was a generous person and touch was a kind of generosity to her. But he came only that one summer. Maybe he died. Or maybe he could not bear to be near her and not have her. Or maybe he went back to sea. He too told stories. He told us that the sound between us and The Calf was haunted. They had all seen a ship there once, in a place where no ship could go because of the shoal. His grandfather had been fishing there another night long ago and whatever he saw or heard he would never say, except that something put a stone in his belly and he failed away, and his skeleton came through his body before he died.

Em was terrified and fascinated by his stories. Once she said to me that she had seen the bones of the fisherman's grandfather. She said Jeannie had brought them wrapped in her sweater and Richard had put the man together on the kitchen table. She still had one of the bones, she said, in a secret place. She wouldn't tell me where it was but I found it easily enough in a hollow in the trunk of an apple tree. There was a brass ring there too, and a metal toy soldier. I left them where I found them. I wonder if they're still there or if the tree has healed over. Trees do that. Some day someone will cut it down and find the bone, the ring and the tin man.

My mother never prayed, she was the least religious person I have ever met, she had not a fingernail of superstition in her, but on the nights of the worst storms she thought the ghosts of the island and the gods of the ruined hearths of the empty houses had turned on her for her betrayals and they would rear the sea up against her and drown her children and herself. We thought it natural for someone to be so fearful. The storms terrified us too. But she was a grown woman. She should have known better.

Whom did she betray? In her grubby flat on the Kingsland Road, in the days when she was quietly planning her escape, she pointed and said, You most of all. Meaning me. And then she named my sisters Jeannie and Em, Richard Wood, herself. She did not mention my father.

She travelled backwards and forwards to the land in our boat. When we heard the distinctive sound of the Seagull engine, the boat coming round Cuas Point and breasting the seas, we would run down to the pier. We wondered what she might bring.

She was an eavesdropper and loved repeating things overheard in the town or on the bus. She had a wry sense of humour. She had her favourite sayings: she got a lovely death, is it yourself is in it, she's out with me over it, he's great with her this past two years, I'm not myself at all, he gave me the going-on strips. They reappeared later in Richard's poems and he was praised for his natural ear. We used to carry the things she bought – fresh vegetables, socks, batteries – as if they were some precious treasure, as indeed all things are on an island. But her to-ing and fro-ing had a darker side too. I recognise it now in retrospect. At the time it did not seem so.

On one trip ashore she found an article in *The Irish Times* that said science was predicting a new Ice Age. She read it to us that evening. She seemed to think the ice was coming soon. She made a list of warm things we had in the house, woollen vests and sweaters, blankets and coats and bobble-hats and mittens and gloves. Then she made a list of things we would need to buy. She was writing at the table and the electricity was out again, but there was enough light in the western sky. She made her list and she wrote it out fair and said we would go to town the next day and draw down whatever my father had put in her bank account and buy the necessaries. Cold would not catch us sleeping, she said, we would be ready. I can see her clearly, writing frantically, rushing around to check that things were where they were supposed to be, talking all the time. Then, for no good reason, she gathered the three of us and sang us a song her mother used to sing. There were three sisters went to school, all around the loney-o, they spied a lady at a pool, down by the greenwood side-o. It was a cruel song and it always frightened us, but we thought of the whole thing as normality, as the way families were, because we had no experience of any other. When the song ended she told me solemnly that when I was inside her she wondered what she would do. She did not want me, she said, but the minute I was born she could hardly imagine how she would do without me. Then she made us all promise that if the ice age came again we would struggle together as a family. She believed that children should be told everything, that they should be treated as adults, that we needed as much information as possible to survive. Next morning there was no more talk of going shopping against the cold. It was a close damp morning and the spiders' nests in the furze were glassy with the night's rain.

She was kneading bread as I came downstairs, watched warily by Flanagan the cat, and she was still humming the song. When she saw me she nipped a piece of dough and held it to me on her finger. It's for you Grace, she said, because you're mine.

She sang:

There is a river wide and deep,
All around the loney-o
'Tis there the babe and mother sleep,
Down by the greenwood side-o.

We three sisters had separate lives. Jeannie liked to build elaborate cities in the sand. She dammed inlets with stones and tried to hold the sea back, anxiously anticipating the rising tide, rushing here and there to stop a hole. Once at low water springs she built a wall across a narrow inlet and packed it with sand. I think the moment she loved best was the breach, the water tumbling in, the crumbling sand and shifting stones. She used to watch it in a kind of anxious ecstasy. I thought she would grow up to build things.

In reality Em was the wildest of us all. I see her now chasing the cat around the house, trying to catch his tail. The cat eventually escapes through an open window. Outside it is late afternoon or early evening. There are seals on the rocks. I can hear their barking. My mother never intended to have her, as she often told us. In fact only Jeannie did not come under that anathema. Em was my accident, she used to say. But neither of us knew how a child could be accidental. Em could walk among the sheep without disturbing them as if she were already a ghost. The cat followed her like a disciple. She brought home an injured blackbird. Look after Em, my mother used to say, and we had to take it in turns, but we were careless and Em was good at hiding. She learned to swim on her own and never told anybody. She might have learned to fly like the shearwaters skimming the waves, but time was against her. She was small enough and her bones were as light as the hollow bones of a bird. I think she was fearless and careless and heedless of everything. I think nothing surprised her. She talked so rarely we never really knew. But sometimes at night she crawled into my bed and slept with her nose between my shoulder blades. In the morning there would be a damp patch in my nightdress. And she slept with her fists bunched as though one day she might need to fight.

I was the curious one. Once I found my father's old store of rabbit snares. Although snaring is mentioned in his first book as a time-honoured way of getting food the outcry from what he called the Cruelty To Everything Except Humans Brigade made him remove it from subsequent editions. Anyway, he had never mastered the technique. Truthfully, he was a poor hunter but he was a good gatherer. They were little hoops of steel with a seized eye spliced into the strands at one end, and a steel peg for anchoring the trap at the other. He may have made them himself. Or the seizing might have been Richard's work, he did his own splicing. All that summer I hunted. I set them at places where the runs went between stones or bushes. I experimented with height. After a time I stopped handling them with my bare hands because I would leave my smell on them. I found a pair of white nylon gloves in my mother's drawer. I decided she didn't need them. I sat on the highest point of the island in the evening when the rabbits came out to play. The frantic movements of a trapped rabbit. The bucking and tearing and slow dying. I skinned them myself, though for a long time I was just hacking and tearing. I only ever managed to cure a single hide. Lying gutted on a plate they looked like dead babies. Their flesh purple under the translucent bitter membrane. Their small mouths. But now I think there was something sexual in the killing and the stripping and in the bare naked flesh with its hind legs spread.

Once I was out on the heather looking at my traps and I saw Jeannie watching me. She didn't know I saw her. She followed me to each trap and watched me kill two rabbits. I got angry when I saw her the second time. I chased her and knocked her down.

What are you snooping for?

I wasn't snooping. I wanted to see how you did it.

I looked at her. She was excited. We had been running of course. Perhaps it was that.

Em never ate them. She frustrated my hunting by finding my traps and stamping on them. Once I caught her trying to free a trapped rabbit. But even she couldn't find everything. And I forgave her.

How long did we live there? How did we get there? In some families there are archivists to record the significant events, but in ours there were none. My mother remembered only what she wanted to remember and what she could not forget and my father committed his memories to paper and never wanted to hear about them again. He wrote them in such a way that they became inventions, remote from our experience. We could not recognise ourselves in them, or more accurately, we tried, and failed, to shape ourselves into them. And in time he stopped writing about us because we could no longer be recycled. This is the inevitable consequence of writing things down.

Certainly, by the time I was old enough to remember things we were already on the island. I remember that they had a gate across the doorway through which I could see the world. When my sisters came along and I was old enough to come and go I saw that this gate was, in fact, a painted fireguard. Where were my sisters born? It is clear that we did not live on the island all the time. There were times when we lived in the city. My mother told me once that my sisters were all born in the old Mother's Hospital in London. I was born there too, she said. It may or may not have been true – she was not entirely reliable at the time. And I never could reconcile it with what I knew of her life.

It's gone now. Years later, when we lived together in her Kingsland flat, we went out to see the building. It looked like a private house. It had the words The Mother's Hospital (Salvation Army) on the front. Why were we born in a Salvation Army hospital? Because that was the way we lived, she said. And that was all she would say. She liked her secrets. The letters, it seems now, were as big as windows. Why did she want to see it? She told me that her three pregnancies were the happiest days of her life. My father was attentive to her, solicitous, and faithful. He was never with anyone else when she was pregnant, and as long as she was breastfeeding he stayed with her. People were so kind. Richard brought her flowers and fruit. When I was born he took her photograph sitting in a pale pink bed-jacket, holding me in her arms. There were apples and roses. He still had that photograph, she said, but she had lost her copy. She was always losing things. She said that we should have been happy children, because her happiness was in her milk. We should have been happy, secure, loving people but we were not. She said she could recall each of our faces exactly as we looked up at her from the breast. Each one was different and beautiful and ancient.

We took the bus out and we went past the stop and got out in Hackney and waited for the next bus back so I saw the place of my birth coming and going and on each occasion all I could think of was my mother's happiness and fulfilment, how having a child at her breast made her feel useful. It was a hurtful discovery. I was angry because in way she was betraying what had happened in the meantime, our grief and our silence. But I kept my anger to myself. It would have served no purpose.

We certainly lived on the island through several springs and summers, and parts, at least, of two winters. We had a boat, an old salmon yawl that took water at a steady pace, steadily sinking all its life. When we got into it there was always water under the boards and sometimes above them. We baled with Heinz bean cans. The engine was a British Seagull Century longshaft that never failed. It smoked and sounded like a machine gun. Mother went out to the mainland, we rarely went with her. She went once a week when she could. Sometimes a boatman came out with things we ordered from the shops. When the weather was bad we stayed at home and lived on short rations. Sometimes our money ran out. Or she gave it away. Occasionally we all went ashore. My mother planned these outings. I remember a tinker woman begging on the street. My mother gave her a ten shilling note – an enormous amount of money. I'm sorry, I have no change. God bless you lady, it's too much.

Or sometimes, with storms building, that particular ominous day before the air fell on the island like a terrified animal, sensing the energy of the coming chaos, we made a run for it and moved ashore for the duration. Crouched in our anoraks, our woolly hats, our wellington boots, our backs turned to the incoming spray and green water, we laughed and thought we were having an adventure. Then we stayed with Richard Wood and watched the rain sweep across the distant rock that was our home. How old was Richard Wood then? He can't have been more than thirty-five, but he seemed to us to be old, as old as the house and its privileges, its ancient arrogant windows. Tiraneering was his house. It means *the land of iron* in Irish. The cat came with us everywhere we went and Richard hated him. I hear him say: I found him asleep in the laundry, He pissed in the kitchen for Jesus sake, That fucking cat ate our supper, You pay more attention to the cat than me. And once he had lambs' kidneys in a bowl on the table and they disappeared – the cat farting urine smells all night. Em laughed at that. Flanagan stinks, she said. But Richard put him outside.

Sometimes father brought us with him to London. He had that Kingsland flat where my mother would eventually die. In those days it was practically in Essex, the furthest bleakest reach of North East London. There was a pub on the ground floor. The railway station was a hundred yards away and there was a kebab house across the street. It was like the centre of the world and we were weary explorers just come from the periphery where we had witnessed marvels too elaborate to tell. We were the sorry end of that peculiar 1960s' invention, the jet-set. We were feckless and lived in several places at once, as they did, but our mode of transport was a salmon yawl, a ferry, a train. We were their inverse image.

At any rate, he *was* famous by then, having appeared on television as the bestselling author.

We heard him more than once on the World Service when we could get it, which depended on the disposition of the atmosphere above our heads, whether we could catch what Richard Wood called the sky-wave or not. We imagined him coursing in on a long swell between the grey and the blue skies, above the clouds. We heard our names.

We thought of him travelling in something very like Richard Wood's *Iliad*. Mother said he was a travelling preacher. She said if ever the world was going to change

28

it would not be because we grew our own vegetables. It would be because people walked away from the bosses. I didn't know who the bosses were.

His stories seemed just like stories to us, like fairy tales. The reality was a few lines of salt-blanched kale. The reality was trying to rot seaweed for fertiliser and having to live with the sour fish smell. Agriculture practiced at the most desultory level. We had no animals except the cat. The reality was being mostly cold at night and then being too hot. And being alone and not knowing how to behave when we were not alone. Of feeling safe with the world's ocean as our moat, a place where no one watched us with envy. A place that was precarious and fatal and temporary. The reality was a kind of foolishness that was like a dream, an existence that had no outside, no edge, that we could never transgress. A dream is a language; it has its own alphabet. But the dream knows that someone somewhere will understand and all communication is founded on that premise. But we grew up without that faith. We never knew that we could be understood. These are the consequences of living on an island.

That last summer I think we sailed almost every day. It must have been an exceptional year. At any rate that's how I remember it. The cockpit of Richard's boat was too small for five of us – Richard Wood, mother, my sisters and I. It was narrow and our feet crossed in the centre and the huge iron tiller extended two feet, so that whoever sat opposite the helmsman might as well have been steering too.

There was one day that I always think of as the beginning of the end. It was time winding up. Of course I believe that the past is not a narrative, it has no beginning and end, even though we survive, we hold ourselves together by telling stories about ourselves. For a practising psychologist I have a weak faith in consequence.

We beat out against a southerly wind and we fished for mackerel all day. We caught only three. The shoals were not in so it must have been June or early July. We hove to about ten miles out and we three children lined the rails and dropped our lines and mother and Richard Wood held their faces to the sun and chatted. When they had enough, he backed the staysail and brought her round and we sailed back, surfing thunderously on the in-going swells. The boat rushed forward, caught in the belly of one, and then, unable to keep pace, slowed and fell back into the following trough. In the valleys the sails flogged and clapped, and on the crest they were full-breasted matrons shooing us home. Mother and Richard Wood took turns at the tiller. They sat very close. I saw that he held her right thigh tightly between his knees. His body was moving with the movement of the boat. Her knee was in his groin.

Her knee in his groin and the motion of the boat and the scissors of his thighs around hers. It was a slow warm day and I was thirteen and at that point it was an easy thing to fall. In those days I swam so much my skin ached. I tasted salt. I was holding the mizzen shroud in one hand and my mackerel feathers in the other. It was simply a matter of transferring my trust from the boat to the line. I fell over the stern. I surfaced quickly. I could feel the tug of the lead. Had a mackerel caught the feather he could have towed me away and I would not have cared. I saw the boat disappear in a trough and when it rose again they were looking for me.

Swimming in the deep sea is a kind of letting go. I could do it because I was never afraid of anything. The darkness was between my legs. I lost a sandal. The boat came back. It was an elegant piece of seamanship. I know he never for a moment believed I had fallen. But I had.

They made me take my clothes off and sit on the bunk in a towel. My mother put the kettle on. Tea would warm me, she said, as she always did. I had given her a fright, but I was a brave girl. She was an innocent, in so many ways, she trusted things to be themselves. My sister Jeannie came down to look at me. She said nothing. My sister Em looked in and asked if I was all right. She too had been worried. Richard watched me from the tiller. I saw that I had moved the stone of his attention. Sunlight slanted in from the porthole. After a time the Primus needed to be pumped again. I did it. When the kettle boiled my mother made tea. There was barely enough room in the tiny cabin for the three of us. She was stooped because the headroom was bad.

They hung my clothes on the guard wire and as we approached the anchorage they gave them back. They were damp and sticky.

Richard said I would need to learn that there was always one hand for the boat and one for myself. He said that I was such an otter I needed to learn how to stay out of the water. I needed to become truly amphibian. I suspected he was preparing a poem in his head and these random metaphors were some kind of a beginning.

Em let the anchor go. She liked lifting the pawl and releasing the clutch with the iron bar. It was something a child could do and love. Lift the pawl and release the clutch and the chain runs out with a satisfying clatter that becomes a growl. Tighten the clutch again. She loved it. The wind was almost gone. We came to a slow stop, winding the jib on the Wykeham-Martin gear. The mizzen was always first to go up, last to come down. It kept her nose to the wind, he said. The bay was ablaze in the evening sun. There was a seal watching us. He put me and Jeannie ashore first and then went back for the others. We walked up to the house.

Jeannie said, I saw you, you jumped.

I did not.

I saw you letting go.

I changed in our room up under the slates and when I came down they were all there in the kitchen. Richard had the mackerel. He ran his knife along the membrane of the belly and the guts spilled out red and black. He nipped the stomach where it penetrated the gut and scraped it into a bucket and started again. My mother had her hands in the basin. She brushed soil from the potatoes with her thumbs. They were laughing. They were talking in low voices but still I heard what they were saying. They were talking about running away. Outside it was already dark. Jeannie was at the window looking out at the reflection of the inside, as though she could see through it. Em was looking into a picture book. Nobody looked at me.

I see now that I was already watching my mother for the secrets she knew, even though in the end it would be Jeannie who mastered them; they were wasted in me. I knew it was her body. I remember her beautiful breasts with their sand-pale aureoles, the wrinkle under them, her full straight thighs and the place between them. Though I didn't know it then, I wanted my body to know such things.

The longer my father stayed away the more open she became with Richard. She kissed him holding her palm flat against his heart. What did her hand hear? I watched them lying in a fold of heather near the beacon facing the sun. She was listening. What was he saying? I would never know. Her summer frock was turned back to her hip. She liked the heat but she never tanned. Her face was freckled but pale. The beacon threw a long shadow. When it reached them they got up.

I listened for their lovemaking all that summer long. But what can be learned from listening tells us nothing about gesture or act. Although what happens is natural enough, no one could invent it exactly. I knew all about whispering and sighing and hushing and the other sounds. Their bed creaked like a boat.

On my birthday, he gave me a poem. Jeannie gave me a stone shaped like a seal with one eye. Em gave me a card with our names in a heart.

We were sitting at the table. I looked at the poem as if I were reading but in reality I was watching my chance. When mother turned to the kitchen I kissed him quickly full on the mouth. It tasted of fat. Mother never saw but Jeannie did. Her jet-black eyes. What was the poem about? I tore it up that night. I never read a word. That night I hated him for sitting there and accepting my kiss and saying nothing to break her spell. When she turned around she was holding my birthday cake on a plate. There were only two candles – I don't think we ever had any more – and he began that idiotic fellow song and they all joined in the chorus. I should have known that he was a failure but children only feel; they have no idea why.

When we had eaten the cake we all went out to see the evening. I remember that the sun was a blood orange and there were thin lines of horizontal cloud. I remember it more intensely because of my state of mind. If it was raining I would remember it as clearly because everything I saw and felt that evening had the intensity of sex. We walked to the western end of the island and my mother, with Richard's help, climbed onto the beacon. She was triumphant and a little crazed. Up there, she said, she would have sunshine long after we were in darkness. Em cried because she was jealous. Em was the climber in the family. I walked down to the pebble beach with Richard. He said, You must take care of your mother, Grace. He was thoughtful, and I think, a little frightened. I knew what he meant. He turned to look back when he said it, and I looked too. She looked like some kind of stone against the darkening sky, a graven image as unsafe and uncertain as any false god.

And then there was a scene in our kitchen some days or weeks later. My mother stood with her back to the sink and her arms folded. She wore, I remember, a long patterned kaftan. The pattern was a kind of red paisley like an amoeba on a pale cream. She wore slacks and sandals. Her hair was tied back by a band of tortoiseshell. She was never more beautiful than when she was angry. Em was somewhere else. She may have been upstairs. Jeannie was sitting by the window. She had been to the well, I remember, and the bucket of water she had brought was standing on the kitchen floor. I could see a fine membrane of dust and pollen and salt gathering on it in the sunlight. Richard Wood stood in the centre of the room talking about me. I needed some discipline in my life, he said. I was growing up. Sooner or later I would leave the island and I would have to make my way in the world. I remember he said it exactly like that, in those old-fashioned terms: I would have to make my own way in the world.

It was as though I weren't there, but I was. Or at least I think I was. It's true that Jeannie remembered it for me. She told me everything in careful detail many years later, including things I didn't know about. She was able to tell me that Richard talked about their plan. He was to take me out sailing and explain everything. He was to do it gently, in a fatherly way, there being no father to speak of at that moment. Out there, alone with me, on the waste of the sea.

Jeannie remembered that he had blue jeans with a slight flare and that he had a faded blue fisherman's smock. He could wear those things authentically. It was as though his class had appropriated the entire history of the country and could be what they liked, whatever character from fiction or history, the poor beggar, the journeyman tailor, the wandering seaman, the sailor. We saw them wherever we went, in London, in the houses we visited, these members of the former ruling class who had adopted victimhood as though it belonged to them.

In the end my mother agreed. She agreed, I think, because she could not do without him. If my father had been there it would never have happened. But there were long weeks when we were alone. When we saw Richard's sails – and they were unmistakeable, two headsails, one set on a bowsprit with the ancient Wykeham–Martin winding gear, the tall mainsail and the little stunted mizzen, the classic yawl-rig, there was no other boat like it on the coast at that time – our hearts lifted. Here was news of the main. Here was someone with stories to tell, with fruit or meat or newspapers or Kiley's lemonade.

All right, she said. I give in. But you must be back by teatime. No wandering.

She meant he could not keep me away after dark. She knew he sometimes drifted up the coast and stayed offshore during the night. That he fished and drank black coffee. That he sometimes found himself among the night trawler fleets, or out where the big companies were prospecting for oil. Or anchored in some cove out of the seaway. She would not stand for that. Not the two of us alone in the boat overnight, the sea and the stars and the two of us in the little cabin in the after-heat of the Primus stove.

I don't think she believed in any plan. Childhood was nothing to her. It was just another time.

So I picked up my anorak, my boots, my jumper and went down with him to the boat.

We would sail south for half the day. At midday we would turn and beat back up. At that point we would be twenty-five or thirty miles offshore. It would be him and me and the deep sea. A sailboat is all protocol and procedure, he said. And the names of things. He named each rope, each stay and shroud, each of the corners of the sails, each edge, each block and its tackle and parts, the sheave, the cheek, the choke, the cleat. He named the processes of taking in and letting go. In the brutal simplicity of that day he named things I have never forgotten. I remember that unless the mizzen was trimmed properly she sailed like a bitch. I remember that he had stitched a leather cutaway into the clew of the inner staysail and the threads had worked loose. I remember that in light airs it was necessary to back the jib to make her tack and that unless it was done smartly the boat simply stopped in irons. All this I learned, and so much more.

The leaving and the return are the boat's best time. She feels the anchor coming home and she becomes impatient for the sea. She is at her slowest and most sensitive. She turns her head. The wind against her body.

First the mizzen. He showed me how to sweat it up. Even for someone with my light frame it was easy work. We unwound the jib and when the anchor was home and dry he allowed her to fall away to one side and used the backed headsail to turn her to the open sea. Once outside the arms of the anchorage he brought her to wind and I sweated the main and the staysail and we bore away. He told me what to do and I must do it at once. There was never to be time to think. I must carry out each order quickly, precisely, calmly. Mistakes would be punished by the boat.

This is what we did.

It was a brilliant day of northerly winds. The sea in the lee of the land was flat. The sails filled and the boat ran out, and all that long day he drove me to distraction.

Far out beyond the horizon there were only two of us. The wood giving to the wind and sea. Wooden boats move in every way.

He told me my mother was worried about me.

His arms around the iron tiller. There was a knuckle of iron at the end. One hand enclosed it.

Did I know that they had talked about sending me to board at his old school? It was co-ed now. My father had been written to. I was a wild child. My mother had asked him to take my reading in hand and so I might be seeing more of him. He said that my father's theories about home schooling were fine when I was younger, but now I would need to sit exams. I would need to think about the future. It was a cruel world, he said, and wildness was punished without mercy. He had been thinking a lot about me, he said, and so had my mother. Worrying, in fact. They had both been worrying about me.

I had not known I was in danger. I sat straight as a larch, staring at the future which seemed to me no more than several wave crests distant. I would leave the island. She wanted to part us. I hated her for it. She was plotting to put me aside. When children think of punishing their parents they understand what it is to be powerless. They think about dying. When I'm dead you'll be sorry. I tried to imagine such a complete punishment. But I also knew I would not be there to know. Then later there was fear. What would school be? What were other people of my age like?

All this as we ran down our southing with nothing but the heaving sea before and the land falling away behind. He watched me. In the dreamy running down when the boat ran almost as fast as the wind and it seemed as if we were carrying our own air, the sails full of it, wing on wing.

I was long and straight from shoulder to hips. My shorts hung low. At some point in my anger and fear I became conscious of the dimpled hollows of back and waist.

His arms wrapped around the iron tiller, his cheek on his shoulder. He had long lashes like a girl's. The sinews of his arms. His hair fell continually into his eyes and he brushed it away with a gesture that took five hundred years to perfect.

And coming back he shouted and hectored me. Each tack was a welter of rope and clattering sail and groaning blocks. We beat up hard-by and water flew in our faces. He worked me brutally, coldly. My muscles hurt. My skin burned from the sheets. Now I know what he was doing. He was loosening my grip on myself.

By evening we were anchored in the Carthys, two broken reefs with a patch of drowned sand between. We were stopping there to eat, he said. In an hour or so the wind would shift and set fair for home. We would coast back on the evening breeze. My mouth was dry. My nails were broken. I was mortally tired. I said I would bathe before eating. I began to change into my swimsuit. I moved swiftly, peeling things away, dropping them. My shirt, my shorts, my pants.

Use a towel, he said. But it was too late.

Look at you, he said, you're brazen.

He smelled of sweat and iron. I was pulling on my bathing suit, I think. I stopped and looked him straight

40

in the eye. What if he kissed me? My head to his? I kept my mouth closed. He would put his hand on me. Now something in my belly leaped like a fish. My heart raced. He looked at my face. I stared brazenly at him, covered barely to the waist, the straps of my bathing suit trapped between finger and thumb of each hand. I saw him look down. I knew what he was looking for. I remembered my mother's muffled cry in the night, the sound of animals struggling. There was an instant that hung at the cusp, when anything might have happened, I believe that still.

Then he slapped me.

I was taut and supple as a whiplash. I went straight out onto the little afterdeck. I thought for an instant of jumping. I believed in swimming away, in striking out for home, five or six miles of open sea. I could trust myself to the ocean. I stretched my arms towards it, arched my back, my toes wrapped on the coaming. Already I was exulting in falling. It would have fixed the moment forever. But he called out.

Don't, he said. Stop as you are.

I turned to defy him. For the first time ever I was conscious of my breasts. They were small – they still are – but the nipples were pale, something like the colour of sunlit sand. It occurred to me that there was power in staying as well as running away.

I'm going to jump, I said.

You'll only have to come back. There's nothing on these rocks.

Someone would come. Mam would come.

41

Who would tell her?

I could swim.

I'll write a poem about you, he said.

He could do the little boy look. He had that grace and simplicity. And he could be sad.

It might have turned my mother's head, but not mine. I shrugged. I didn't like poems. He had left several in our house for safe-keeping at various times. They were memorials of his days here, vignettes of our lives, love poems to a family that was not his. I didn't think they were important. We always lost them.

He said, You could be a boy or a girl.

I didn't know how to understand that. Was it good or bad? What I felt was shame.

I shook my head.

Come and put your clothes on. Let's go home.

Put your clothes on, he said again.

I sulked. But I didn't jump. He nodded once, as though he had read my thoughts. I watched him go below.

My eyes were heavy. Everything went in phases, slow as water. He pumped the Primus. The sharp smell of the paraffin. The pop of the flame. My legs felt too long, like an animal's. An eland or a gazelle. And we sat at opposite ends of the cockpit. We had bread and cheese and tea. I folded one knee onto the other as my mother did, slanted my legs away. It was a warm still evening. The breeze that would take us home was slow in coming. He watched me from under his lashes. I felt free and dangerous as though *I* had hurt him. When the night breeze finally blew I left that reef full of pleasure and power. I remember standing on the bow of the *Iliad* with my legs spread, braced to the inner forestay, the wire pressed into my skin. Afterwards my arm and side were flecked with tar where the strands left their mark. The breeze was in my face then. If he had asked me I would have given him everything. It might have been a world, a universe, a way of life – I didn't know what would be required of me, but I knew it was vast. There were no discernible tracks. The mountain sheep knew the way, those that came to the island. The seabirds on the cliffs knew. The seals, the dolphins, the fin whales. Their sinuous bodies found the seaway without pain. Now I wanted to know more than anything what his body would feel like. What would come next? Where would he go?

Later Jeannie told me that they had talked about me and that my mother said I was becoming a woman. I said I thought that's what I had always been, that it just meant I wasn't a man. But Jeannie instinctively knew that it was something else, something more important and that there was something dangerous in it, that I should be afraid. When I didn't react she told me it was raining outside and did I want to play draughts? She listed the other games we could play. Ludo, Snakes & Ladders, Dominoes, Junior Scrabble which mother was keen on but we were not. I ignored her. I was pretending to be reading, but I knew that Jeannie was right. This would be my last year of freedom. I knew all about schools. I had read *The Highland Twins At The Chalet School* and *Hard Times*. There was something cold and hard in the pit of my stomach that must have been dread. *Facts, facts, facts* – that was the future to which I would never belong.

She jumped on the bed beside me. She knew what she was doing. She was always the bringer of bad news. She leaned over my shoulder so that her face was against mine. Her skin was dry and hot. Her breath smelled yeasty.

They're sending you away, she said. They're going to send you to school.

My father never came all that remained of the summer and my mother, as I remember it, never once spoke about him. Nor did she mention school. I came to believe that if I was a good girl nothing more would happen. I could stop the arrow in flight.

All this happened to us as I remember it, things we had no right to expect, wonders and minor miracles and also terrible things. We children tried to find our way in this world of edges that proliferated into chaos, and I suppose the adults were navigating too. Only the cat knew everything.

Four

It's Grace's day to look after Em. She and Em are down at the western beach searching for soft-belly crabs under stones to bait hooks with. They had a bucket for them and the bucket was filling with scrabbling green and brown machines. It's a summer's day. I'm wandering on the western end of the island looking for bright stones or bits of quartz. I find the bones of a seabird in a wall. I brush the bones out with a feather they're so light. They're chalk fine, so fragile I think they might turn to dust in my hands. I brush them onto my sweater, lay them out on the heather below and begin to put them together again. I feel a terrible sense of loss as if the bird is mine, a pet or one that was nesting under my window. Birds, like humans, seek out shelter in bad times. We all need a niche in a wall to hide ourselves in, to get well again, or to die. I'm so lost in setting the bones back in place that I miss the clouds building out from the mainland, the distant thunder. When the downpour begins I'm taken by surprise and for a time in the noise and the battery of the rain I'm completely lost. Eventually I bundle the bones into my sweater and run for home.

Richard is there.

Jane is lying down upstairs.

He laughs. Look at you, we have to get you out of those clothes, you'll catch your death of cold.

He peels them off one by one and wraps me in a towel and I stand there like a stick insect, a gangly bony shivering child and he holds me tight and scrubs me. All our towels are ruined by salt. They're coarse and unbending. I think he scoured my skin away and penetrated to my heart. He could have seen it beating steadily, contentedly, if he had bothered to turn me round.

When I'm dry he kisses me on the top of my head and slaps my bottom. Get into something dry, he says, go on now you silly child. Words of endearment. Sometimes he calls me that still. Come here to me silly child.

When I come out again he's opened my bundle of bones. He's spread the sweater on the kitchen table and Grace is there and they're speculating about the structure and function of the bits and pieces. The bones in their hands. This one fits here. If we put that there then these two go together. Suddenly I hate her. I stand there and watch her taking my place and I have nothing to say. Em comes over to watch too; her thumb in her mouth, she studies the bones. The rain outside the window is straight down without wind to slant it, a grey curtain that closes off the entire ocean. The air in the house feels colder and cleaner. I go upstairs and pick up one of Grace's books. I can't remember what it was now, she was always reading. I climb onto a chair and open the roof window and put the book outside on the slates. The sea is furious, explosive, frightening. A storm is happening far away. The effects come here to move the stones and break the cliffs down. The small cove is full of water even though it should be only half-tide. There's a boiling yellowish scum all along the edges, sticks, seaweed, a glass pot-buoy, a milk crate. Rain. The house is drowning in static. The light becomes steel. The blank windows.

Flakes of memory from a nugget of malachite that is the unknowable past. But none of us has a whole memory anyway, whatever we think. What we hear others tell us permeates our understanding. Their thoughts run like subterranean streams in ours. Never trust anyone who has a simple tale to tell.

Jeannie loves stones – I've heard them say that about me since I was a child. It usually feels like a joke, something complicated implying that I find it hard to love people. But of all the family, I'm the lover, the faithful lover of people. Still, it's true stone is my passion. When I was a girl I wondered why in certain places the rocks lay flat, in others sloped and in others curved, why some stones are round and others sharp. These are simple questions but the answer is as complicated as the history of the world. Before ever I came to study geology I'd formed my own theories about how the ground under my feet came to be. Once in a second-hand bookshop I found a topological map and saw that a great wave-train of Old Red Sandstone ran along the coast to the west of our island, with spatters of limestone in the troughs; I saw that the tops of this wave-train were the headlands that I could see marching westwards into the sunset, and that the troughs were the bays that the sea had hollowed out of the soft limestone. It was years before I confirmed this impression in a textbook and when I did I was disappointed to find that the theory was not my own, but also quietly pleased at having discovered it for myself.

I was always fascinated by the tides. Where did they start? Why did the moon change them? Richard knew. He drew diagrams at the kitchen table, circles and sine waves and arrows. The great tide-wave of the Atlantic runs from the North Cape of Norway where the Atlantic and Barents seas meet, past Fastnet Rock to the south of us, and back again every six hours, billions of tonnes of water grinding against the continents and islands – a wave a hundred feet high was recorded not far from our island and they say it was not unusual. This vast swirl of water washes the stones at our door and sweeps the ocean bed clear. We lived, in those days, in an iron-bound coast with deep safe harbours, a morphology shaped by folding and fracture as well as by erosion and hydraulic action; we lived in the presence of big round mountains that rose in the distance, old worn mountains shaped by rain and wind, among the islands and their outlying reefs, their sands and their pebble beaches and raised beaches and the fragile remains of human habitation.

Another flake of malachite.

Tom is leaving the island tomorrow. Tonight there is the preparation. Mainly he travels with only a large rucksack for his clothes, his manuscript, whatever he was working on at the time. He keeps the manuscript in a plastic bag. I remember that it was a faded olive-green Marks and Spencer's bag. He used to say that Marks and Sparks did the best quality plastic. Of course it's raining. His oilskins hang stiff as corpses behind the door, ready for the crossing. Em hides her top half behind them and every once in a while looks out to see if anyone has noticed. When she looks I make a face at her and she smiles that slow secret smile. Peek-a-boo.

Recriminations.

Jane says, I can't manage on my own. When will you be back? What am I going to do for money? Easy for you to say. Do you have any idea what it's like?

Daddy, can I come this time, you promised.

My sister Grace looks on. I think I can feel her contempt but that's probably something I've invented over the years. Certainly she hated all of that. It's possible that she hated Tom even then. When he was around she would refuse to eat and he would make her and there was that childish game of denial and withholding that she probably knows all about now. Even then I knew it was just a way of getting his attention.

49

Flanagan stares from his perch on the window, his insouciant eyes say: However it falls out I'll be fed.

Please Daddy…

Suddenly I see weeks that are like years stretch out before me. Islands are, more than anything else, places of deprivation. How old am I? Six, seven?

I want to go, I want to go, you promised.

I have seen children winding up like that, the mantra of wanting and needing and deserving. In a few minutes it will become a wail. He slaps me. I hear it first and feel it later. It can't have been very hard, he never used force.

Jane says nothing. She sits at the table, the mother figure of a demented folk-story, her hair tangled, her fingernails outlined in black, her cheesecloth shirt stiff with salt.

Grace sniggers.

Em winds into his arms and begins to cry.

Following her example I cry too.

I'm sick of here, I wail, I want to go.

Why don't you take her, Jane says.

One of these days…

There's no time like the present.

Jesus Christ, this is a madhouse.

Please Daddy…?

He sits Em on a free chair and kisses her on the cheek. He gets up and goes to the door. The door is open because the rain is soft and the night is cloying-warm. The sea is still out there. In the distance we can hear the foghorn on Fastnet Rock.

He turns suddenly and there is his warmest smile. It radiates everything I ever wanted – love, happiness, comfort, hope. Oh he was a charmer, he charmed thousands in every corner of the world. I was a child – how could I resist. Come here to me child, he says. He holds his arms out and I run for them. He wraps them round me.

What will I bring you from America, he says. Will I bring you a red Indian?

Laughing and smothered, held tightly in the oily, sheepy smell of his Aran sweater, I hear Grace's step on the stairs and the door of our room closing.

Oh you can win them over when you want to, Jane says, easy done when you're only here a few weeks in the season. You don't have to scratch a summer out of this fucking rock. I can't cope any longer. Put that in your next bloody book. It doesn't work, Tom. I'm not going to live the way you want.

I turn in the wheel of his embrace and look at her. I want her to come into the circle too. She is tapping the table with her middle finger, sharp short raps like a blackbird breaking a mussel shell on a rock. Suddenly she sweeps her hand away and a plate and a cup fly. They break against the wall. She looks at them for a moment, then she begins to rap again.

The watchtower is another sombre flake of green in my box of memories.

I go there to play a game I call chainies. This game never includes Grace because Grace is outside everything.

I don't know where I learned the game. It was as if games grew naturally from the landscape and their names were inherently exact. I have bits of old china, broken plates and saucers, cups without handles, but also certain beautiful stones and pieces of sea-worn glass. I have fragments of those old glass buoys they used to mark lobster pots, the most beautiful green blasted to jade by the action of the sea. Sometimes my chainies are things in a shop. Sometimes I serve tea in them to my menagerie of toys, a bear with one eye, a donkey without a tail, a small monkey. I've trodden down something like a hare's form inside the ruined walls of the watchtower, the weeds all laid out in the anti-clockwise direction I first walked them. There's no wind in there. Sometimes I hear a gale grumbling over the walls, the sea grinding against the cliff. I see seabirds blown away on the wind's wings. But inside is my own private calm, a constant storm's eye, my own world.

I hear a noise. I turn and look to the entrance but there's no one there. Then I see her shadow. Em's shadow. She is perched high on the wall looking down at me. How did she get there? The memory is unsettling. It has no clear beginning or end. Was she there before I arrived? Have I forgotten or repressed some decision to allow her to climb on the forbidden wall? I can't be certain anymore. It has the logic of a nightmare. In memory I am paralysed by her presence. She sits beside the window with its musket loop, kicking her heels against the stone. Don't go any further, Em. The window is a whirlpool of emptiness: none of us has passed it. Our heads whirl at the thought.

She doesn't acknowledge that I see her. She is watching the game. She has her thumb in her mouth. Her eyes are big. A child's game is a closely defined world. To step outside for an instant is to see the world vaporise like a dying star.

You're meant to be with Grace, I say, it's her day.

She says nothing, but she inches down on her bottom and runs away.

But Grace plays games too. She invents one that only she can win. First she promises something: to tell something, because she always knew secrets; to give something; to do something. I always want what she has to offer. Then she explains something difficult or unpleasant that I must do to get it. The pleasure she takes in watching my agonised desire, my bargaining, my reluctant acceptance. Grace's game is what passes for fate in my childhood. She knows where a robin is nesting. There are three eggs. If I want to see it I have to tell Jane a lie. I spend days trying to invent a lie that I would be able to tell. Then she brings me to see the nest. She always keeps her promise, that's part of the game. Strands of my black hair and Grace's fair are wound together with grass and leaves and, in the middle, three perfect eggs the colour of sandstone. If you mind Em I'll show you the hole where the conger comes out.

That summer there is a great bloom of jellyfish all along the south and west coast. They wash in on the sand and we bury them above the tide line. They are our aliens, palmfuls of coloured glass and string. Grace swims and occasionally emerges with little weals of sting. She will tell me a secret, I forget what now, if I come too. From a distance she looks like she's floating on a vast sheet of coloured glass. I am too frightened. At night they give me bad dreams. They come and go on the tide, the earth's phlegmy breathing. Then one day they're gone forever and it is autumn.

Jane is trying to school us. On one of her trips ashore she picks up a book about the sea. She wants to use the jellyfish to make us learn. It is an admirable theory of education. Among other things she tells us that they have two phases, the polyp and the medusa, and they reproduce by budding; the life cycle is characterised by pulses which give rise to summer blooms like the one coming ashore on our strand. But information comes to us as a kind of pleasant static from another country, inexplicable, a cipher for which we have no key but which is beautiful to contemplate. Gradually I lose my fear. If the bloom returned now I would do it and Grace could tell me the secret she never revealed. Em has fallen in love with the words. She has a little song she sings that goes Polyp, medusa, bloom, polyp medusa bloom. She sings it over and over again. I hear her singing herself to sleep.

One day a boy comes ashore from a lobsterman's boat. They have engine trouble. I see them pulling into the western beach, running the bow onto the shingle. It is a dangerous entrance, a sharp reef with a narrow gap. Only a local could find his way in. Together they take the cowling off the outboard and begin taking it apart. They spread an oilskin coat on the shingle and place the pieces on it. Flanagan the cat comes down. Whenever a boat lands he suspects fish. He lounges in the sea-pinks watching and dozing. After a time I see that the boy has nothing to do. I go down and ask him if he wants to play. I was a wild child with no idea how to behave with strangers. His father stares at me, but the boy says yes. I'm pleased because he's a big boy and little girls are in awe of big boys.

I bring the boy to the tower and show him my treasures. I explain the game but I can see that he's not concentrating. I scold him for not paying attention. He asks me to show him my knickers. I don't care about knickers but I know the game would never work that way. I refuse and when he tries to catch me I dodge past him easily and up onto the wall. He starts to climb after me. Then he sees the sheer drop on his left-hand side, a hundred feet or more from where we stand to the sea. The water below is clear. He stops climbing.

He tries to get me to come down. I think he's more frightened now than interested in my underwear. From high up over the sea I lift my skirt and show him my knickers and then I stick my tongue out and laugh at him. It is Grace's laugh, the way she can make me feel small. He runs away. I can see him tearing through the thistles and bracken.

I'm excited. For a long time afterwards I tried to think why he wanted me to show and why he thought I would.

We're at Richard's house at Tiraneering. Grace is reading, Em is sleeping in Jane's arms, Richard is closing the big shutters with their brass latches. Tom is there but I do not see him in memory. It's late and we have been playing cards. Who won? It was usually my father. But I cannot remember.

Then we go upstairs, Tom, Grace, Em, Jane, Richard and I, turning out the lights one by one so that by the time we reach the top of the stairs there is a huge fissure of darkness at our backs with black Flanagan the cat emerging from it, his eyes of malachite green. He sleeps with Jane.

These old houses, Richard used to say, they need an empire to keep them alive. Meaning the portraits of admirals and colonels who went out to defend England in the China Sea and Omdurman. This is Captain Richard Wood, he was with Nelson at the Nile, he was wounded in the leg by a fragment of iron from the explosion of *L'Orient*. I loved those stories. Between the colonels and admirals, the dead aunts mostly disapproving of what had befallen them − death and reduced circumstances, retirement, half pay, the Encumbered Estates Act.

The stupidity of memorial.

Tom standing on the top step with his hands resting on the balustrade, declaring his objections to all of that: We should have burned you out like foxes.

Flanagan is cat-sniffing around his feet, his greeting ritual. Does that mean Tom has just arrived? Where has he come from? How long have we been here?

And Richard saying, Nobody burns foxes out Tom.

My father means the War of Independence, that all the landlords should have been driven away. He's against land ownership, or at least ownership on the vast scale of the Tiraneering estate. Now they're at it hammer and tongs: the landlord class, the gombeen class, parasites, reactionaries.

Arguments terrify a child. I've no concept of what a friendly quarrel might lead to, how friends make fun of each other. To me it looks and sounds like Grace's game. I have no skin. I'm always sensitive, in so many ways, whereas Grace has a professional hauteur that protects her from the vagaries of love.

Later I can't sleep. I think about fire. I look at the windows to see how they can be opened. I wonder would I die if I jumped out onto the stone yard below. There's moonlight, that night or another night, and I see an owl ghosting towards the fields. He seems inflated, enormous. I don't know what he is – I think he might be a soul taking leave of us.

That night or another night there are words about Jane. I don't know what is said – they're always talking riddles.

It is Em who wakes us. She says she heard a ghost. She lies in Grace's bed with her eyes wide open, her thumb in her mouth. It's possible only she knew how things would turn out: children and dogs, they say, have that instinct. We listen but hear nothing. Then it comes again, a faint, animal wailing. Then there are doors. First we are happy that the sound is human, then we realise that the silence means we are alone. We close the shutters but it does no good. We hear Flanagan mewling at the door and let him in. We are all terrified but Grace is the worst. Poor Grace. Why is it that without seeing we all know the sequence? They argued, mother cried, she walked out. It is a dark cold night. There is no moon and the stars are like broken glass.

We go over the sequence, folding our stories into each other: Grace says there was the wailing and then loud talk and then shouting, I remember the kitchen door banging closed, then there was silence, we are all agreed on that, we all remember the silence. Grace says she heard Jane's voice in the yard so we all go to the window and open the shutters again to look down. We are in time to see Tom and Richard carrying flashlights, going their separate ways, Richard through the gate, Tom by the side of the old stable. They are calling and calling, for a time we can see their lights.

Grace says that if they want to find her they have to leave us alone. If we want our mother back we must wait in the haunted room. Grace is playing one of her games, I know, but I'm still frightened. Em begins to cry. Mammy is gone, she keeps saying, mammy is gone.

58

Grace holds her in her arms. She'll come back Em, she says.

Old houses, big houses make noise, they talk at night in their own fabric language. A million beetles eat. Mice live in the attics and behind the wainscot. Rafters and runners and boards shift in their beds of stone. Lath and plaster wear each other away. Water courses in copper and lead. Every time the house settles itself we hear a pistol shot, a groan. We hear ghosts in the other rooms. Conversations. Noises on the landing.

We fall asleep together – children need sleep more than love and Flanagan is our comforter – Em between Grace and me, none of us knowing what we fear, but fearing that when we wake up everything will have fallen apart, everything will be different. At such times a continuation of even the unhappiest life is preferable to the unknown. We dream of course, whatever those dreams were, certainly uneasy versions of ourselves. At some point Flanagan gives up and moves out. None of us are awake to hear them bring her back, but in the morning she's there to wake us. It's no comfort. She's pale and her eyes are red. For all we know she might be a changeling, a fairy woman. For all we know our mother might have gone into the bog and this is her ghost.

Our island home. What is the house like?

Go through the front door and you're immediately in the kitchen. Flanagan checks your shoes for hostile tomcat smells; he knows there is no other cat on the island. He knows me. You may pass Jeannie, his insouciance says, you're nothing new. This is the biggest room, with the chimney breast at one end and the stairs to 'the loft' at the other. Before we came someone put a black Stanley No.8 range in the chimney and when it is hot it heats the entire house. Tom told me that when they bought the house there were mice nesting in the oven. They scampered out when Jane opened the door. She just laughed.

The timbers that hold up the floor above us are solid oak, they look like ship's timbers, and the floorboards above are oak planks too. There is a long tradition of harvesting shipwrecks along this coast. In *Living An Island, Loving The World* Tom told about seafaring families who buried timber or brass or furniture or brandy and the complicated folk-laws that governed found things. It was his most popular book.

Up the narrow stairs, Flanagan at our heels, and there are two bedrooms, each with a 'light', a window set into the roof that mainly looked upwards at the sky. Their room has an iron-framed double bed which they kept because Jane said it would be bad luck to throw out. It's heavy cast-iron with brass knobs and where it stands there are four hollows in the oak made by the casters. Flanagan sleeps in the bed, and on bad nights he sleeps underneath among the shoes and cardboard boxes of winter clothes.

Our room has three iron-framed beds, hospital issue, which they picked up when a local hospital was downgraded to an old-folks home. Although the windows are set into the slope of the roof still by standing close to them I can see down to the shore and across the sound at the sandbar where oystercatchers and turnstones, curlews and sandpipers lived their intertidal days. Wading birds feature strongly around us. Their cries are our nightsongs. Em imitates them. She can do a curlew perfectly. She could call them here from the half-tide flats but what would we do with them?

To furnish the house Jane and Tom and Richard scour the auction rooms. The Irish are throwing out their old mahogany to buy expensive stuff veneered with Formica and there's a ready supply of what people eventually begin to talk of as 'antiques'. To Tom and Jane they're just the cheapest, strongest, most functional things they can get. One day they buy a deal table for the price of a shirt (Tom's words) and beech chairs, a pine dresser, an oak log-box and a coal scuttle with a cracked tin lining. Another evening they come home in an over-laden salmon yawl and disembark a mahogany armchair, a rose-wood lady-chair and a bevelled mirror in an art-deco frame. In a priest's house, being sold as part of the reforms of the Second Vatican Council, they find a brass-bound barometer and a perfect mahogany sideboard to be shipped out to us in a trawler a week later so that its legs smell of sour fish for weeks. We're picking up the Pope's cast-offs, Tom says.

They speak of it as furniture but later I recognise it as a political position: they're rejecting capitalism, or at least Jane is, the conventions of rising consumerism, the faith in the new, in favour of the products of unalienated labour. Others might have fetishised the old, the antique. Not Tom and Jane. It's more of an anachronism now than it was then. In those days there were people like that.

Even as a child I'm fascinated by Richard's body. All the things he did were perfectly elaborated, every action was exact and sufficient. Even the process of swallowing something – a piece of fruit, a sip of whiskey – is beautifully faithful to itself. I long to be as self-contained in everything, to be Miss Jean Wood and not Jeannie Newman, child of the Big House and not a ragamuffin on an island. When I see him naked for the first time – at seven or eight – I experience none of the shock that children are supposed to feel. Instead I see his leanness, his hair, his sex, his long fingers and loose limbs for what they are, in their proportions, expressions of his personality, the physical poetry of his mind. He's swimming with Jane in the moonlight on a completely calm sea. They're making no sound. It's such a night that even if there were ripples I would hear them. It is, I think, the beach near Tiraneering because there are pebbles underfoot. I don't see them go into the water but I see their heads, the slow gleam of their path, the occasional white arm in the air. When they come back I see he is a god, in the pale moonlight he might be stone. That he should quarrel with Tom over everything was perfectly reasonable then. When they come out, it's Jane who wraps him in a towel. She folds her arms around him as if she were sheltering him. She whispers into his ear. Everyone knows that something whispered directly into your ear is more exciting, more devastating. It is absorbed like oxygen across the blood–brain barrier. There's no defence.

Her hair is long and it hangs wet down her back to her shoulder blades. They turn and I know that they will discover me if I stay where I am. But if I stay I will see more. I can hear Grace's voice in my head. What will they do next? What happens now? Stay and learn the secret and be caught. I run home. By the time they get back I'm in bed practising the lies I will tell if they notice anything. But they think I'm asleep. Jeannie sleeps like the dead, Jane used to say.

I may be mistaken – it's too late now to know whether the two incidents were really one, the night-swim and the first seeing of his body, and I've never dared to ask him. They both belong to the primordial mass of childhood. They are available to me only in this singular form, like erratics carried by glacial time and deposited on this highland. But their meaning for me is crystal clear, reason enough to remember them out of all the blizzard of experience. They mean fear and lust.

Fear and lust.

So I suppose Richard was my first love. His image set in me, stony and recalcitrant as the perfect man, the perfect lover. Some girls fall in love over and over again with variations on their father. Grace would make much of that, it's the psychologist's perfect love affair. But I skipped whatever necessary anguish was required and fell in love with my father's best friend. A misdirected Oedipal urge? A transfer of affection from the taboo subject? I find psychology tiresome, a kind of literary criticism of dreams and chance utterances masquerading as science. The chemical formula for calcium carbonate is $CaCO_3$. Show me a single observation in psychology that's as clear as that. There are none. Science has thousands.

Here is something that I remember in exact detail: it's the morning after the night-swim – or possibly a different morning. I go into Richard's room and slip into his bed and put my arms around him. I can hear Jane downstairs putting crockery on the table for breakfast. He's asleep on his side. He loosens a little under my grasp. He rolls back into me. The moment of surrender. I'd seen Jane wrapped into Tom like this, Tom opening to her. I'd seen her wheedling him on the strand, tickling his nose with a sea-pink, curled into his back with one hand plucking at the hairs of his chest.

I know exactly what I'm doing.

His body warm and musty and full of nightsmells.

Then he senses my smallness and wakes up. How, in his sleep, did an impression of my body form? Did he dream of a child? He wakes and is cross. What are you doing, get out, out of here, go on, what are you doing …

I was too young to be able to read the look on his face. Now I wonder what it was. Was he shocked? Frightened? Ashamed? Angry? Hurt? Excited?

He may have thought it was some childish and inappropriate game.

I go back to my own bed.

As I lie shivering in the morning sheets I feel nothing but triumph. I've done something. Something has happened. Children rarely have the feeling that they can cause things. They experience the world as happening to them. I feel as though I've appropriated something of Jane's power. Now I'm a witch too.

He never told anyone.

But later that day – I'm certain of this – he asked me to walk with him. He is going out to meet the farm manager and to see about cattle. It's a September day of showers and sun and we climb gates and cross fields as happy as birds. I remember that I talked a lot. We meet the farm manager and while they walk among the cattle I pick mushrooms. Richard lends me his cap to bring them home. On the way back we disturb a cock pheasant. He rises out of a lane with a clattering like some wild machinery. He flies over our heads, that strange impossibly heavy and ungainly flight of the pheasant and his amazing barred gold and russet plumage, and disappears into the woods. Richard tells me that the place is called Derrybeg and that in Irish it means the small wood. He says there is a little sheltered beach nearby called Derrynatra, which means the wood of the beach, and that the sound between the islands that we can see from where we stand is called Derrynatra Sound. Even then I saw the system of it, and that in one language the place made complete sense and in another it was just noise. I never forgot the relationship between language and landscape. Years later I remember being asked by a colleague how to find a particular geological feature in a place called Mullock. Look for a hill, I said. *Mullach* means a hill.

Richard and I hold hands walking home in the evening sun and I have never been happier before or since. We talk about what we see. It's Eden and there would never be a fall from grace. The world would always be warm in autumn and I would always be a child and he would be kind. That was how I felt that evening. It was Keat's Ode – but the Grecian Urn – *Ah, happy, happy boughs! that cannot shed / Your leaves, nor ever bid the Spring adieu.*

But also it's the knowledge that going into his bed had provoked this excess of kindness.

A storm comes with heavy rain. We are at home on the island. None of us goes outdoors all day. Usually when that happened there were games but Jane and Tom aren't speaking. Jane is reading in bed. Tom sits at the table under the window, alternately writing and staring at the rain. Em plays with her toys in her concentrated way.

At some point in the morning Jane comes downstairs. She sits beside Em and puts her arm around her.

Did you get your breakfast Em?

No.

Did you get your breakfast Grace?

No mam, not yet.

She rounds on Tom. His back is to her. She stands looking at him for a while. The gloomy shabby room full of second-hand things, the clock, the crooked table, the worn shawl that covered the obscene stuffing of the lady-chair, the earthen uneven floor, the leaking stove. I realise I'm ashamed of the way we live.

Tom doesn't turn.

You're useless, she says. This is my island, my house. For you it's only an experiment.

Grace looks at me. What does she know? Being a child means never knowing what other people know. I notice that Tom keeps his head down. An ocean is raining down outside, an inversion of the natural order. I would not be surprised to see fish nosing at the glass, or a seal curious about what happens in houses.

Are you going to grace me with a reply, she says. She waits a while.

That's your answer then?

Tom is silent. What question is it an answer to? What did they say to each other last night after we fell asleep? In the world of adults everything is bigger. There are things that can never be said although children say them all the time: I hate you; I'm going to kill you; I'm going to spit on you.

Fine, she says, I know where I stand.

She walks out into the rain. She doesn't close the door. She never did when she walked out. I see that she's wearing a shirt and a short pants. I call out to her, Mam your coat! But she doesn't respond. She doesn't care. It's her island, her home. She'll walk where she likes. For the first time I understand that she doesn't need Tom. The wind drives the rain across the floor. The earth will be mud but the house will still stand, the island holding it together. Grace closes it out.

I saw Jane kill a hen by wringing its neck.

There is a terrible moment of stillness when she pins the bird's wings. I see that the bird is paralysed by fear, unable to comprehend this new turn of the world. The eyes brown and black, black at the centre. I'm frightened to be so close. This frantic mechanism, this heart and talon and feather construction. It smells musty and domestic. She clasps the bird to her breast and with her right hand she finds the neck and, holding the skull in the cup of her palm, twisting her hand in advance so that the movement would be completely natural, she stretches it out and she kills it. There is some fluttering afterwards but nothing much else. The ghost of life remains but the thing is gone. My mother did that without a thought.

Grace has that same pitilessness. I see her with a seagull trapped in one of her rabbit snares. First she tries to catch the bird but it flies at her. Then she kills it with a stone. She detaches the snare and throws the dead bird into a field. I never see her mourn a single dead thing.

There are things I can recall with precision, like when a slide comes into focus in the microscope, a simple adjustment bringing to life a universe in the objective lens. Trivial things come most readily. I remember how clear the sea is on calm days. A distorting mirror. I remember the brackish taste of well water after a storm. I remember Em's thumbnail soft and white from sucking while her other fingers have a fine black sickle under each nail. I remember how Richard hauls a fish straight up out of the water on his hand line and lands it into a bucket, how he inserts his thumb and forefinger into the gills to break its neck. And the crooked cock of the head relative to the body. I remember Grace throwing herself on the bed, exactly how she pouts when she says I'm stupid, how thin she is, her body straight as a fish. I can see her now. The sea has its own light, a blink of brightness. There is always sea in the light of an island. She lies on her bed in our house, constructing her dilemmas. Richard and mother and Em are downstairs. Richard's boat is anchored in the bay.

Whales are following the tide.

Seals are moaning.

The stones face the ocean impassively, never suspecting that the ocean will win.

It is that time.

Five

Then my sister Emily died. She fell from the watchtower. She was scrambling on the stones of the wall.

Jeannie said that Em had taken to following her, that she was always in and out of the tower.

Later the coroner would say that she had injured herself on the way down, that her back was broken too. Richard Wood and my father made the story straight for him. He praised their clear concise evidence and expressed his sympathy with the family. A childhood accident, he said. He quoted the Bible. They know not what they do. They never asked me. At that time I had other ideas, though I came to believe their story.

I was the one who found her. I should have been taking care of her. But I knew where to look. I brought her ashore. Richard Wood was not there. My mother waited at the pier. I carried Em to her and gave the child into her hands. Then I pushed the boat into deeper water and started the Seagull. I went for the doctor and the lifeboat and I phoned Tiraneering from the public box above the pier. They got to the island before me.

My mother wanted to bury the child there but it was against the law.

Laws of interment are ancient instruments. They are designed to prevent contagion, disease and theft. They only *appear* to be concerned with dignity, love, hospitality. In reality a grave is a piece of property like any other. It is a small piece of land into which a child is put. It has a stone with the child's name. Time elapsed is recorded. It is a complete archive. It contains flesh and bone and memory and the parentheses of birth and death. And in the end, like most property, it is owned by someone other than the occupant. It is a mortgage on the past.

The coroner pieced together a narrative of her death for us.

We experienced it as a piece of fiction, less credible in fact because it had no internal order, no structuring principle. We fell apart. The world fell apart.

But the coroner's enquiry could not touch us.

My memories were useless and, in fact, I was already forgetting. It would take me thirty years to remember my part in it. I could tell how she slept with her nose to my back. How she held my mother's hand when she was talking to her, looking up at her face and just holding her hand like a toy. Those things cast no light on the matter, though he listened to them patiently enough.

My mother remembered. She gave evidence in a tight hurt voice, like a frightened child reciting last night's homework. Even I could see that she was in danger of falling apart, or that she had already fallen apart and been put together the wrong way. She kept looking at my father and he nodded and smiled at her.

This is what she said. Em had been with her in the kitchen. It was teatime. It was my day. Then Em was gone. Where is that notice-box of a child? And where is Grace? I'll have to go after her. Then she broke down and cried. The coroner gave her tissues. He seemed to have a box ready just in case. Perhaps coroners always do.

In time she continued. She told them that she knew something terrible had happened.

Everyone looked for her.

I was the one who saw her. I climbed the watchtower wall because it was the highest thing on the island. From the height of the tower I saw her drifting in the submarine currents, among the white and rounded shale from the last cliff-fall. She wore blue dungarees and a pink and white striped shirt and one blue rubber dolly. Her hands were outstretched.

She sometimes slept like that too, face-down in her bed.

Part Two

Six

We left the island. I went to school and then university. My sister Jeannie went with my father. Richard Wood published a book. My mother had her first breakdown.

Time passed.

My father divorced my mother and married again. He married her opposite.

We lived in the flat in the Kingsland Road. My mother and I.

Where there had been days there were years.

So one day I took the train from Waterloo to Portsmouth Harbour and then the Red Funnel Ferry. I was looking for my father. I glanced back on the crossing and saw that I was leaving a vast industrial harbour. There were warships at anchor. It was a summer's day and sailing boats were working up with the tide. There was a yawl there. She had a high-clewed yankee and a staysail. I saw how they trimmed the mizzen hard to keep her nose to it. The man at the tiller wore a blue yachting cap. He was lean and long-limbed. He wore faded red trousers and a blue fisherman's smock. I watched him until he was too far away.

My sister Jeannie met me at the pierhead. I tried hard to recognise her in the waiting crowd but it was she who picked me out. In five years or six years she had turned into a sullen beauty. In the breakdown of our lives she got my father and I got my mother. She got dark hair and I got fair. She got a perfect complexion and I got freckles. She was sixteen, I was twenty. She opened the boot for me to put my bag in and left me to close it. Her car was an Anglia. She drove with determination and uncertainty along the waterfront and up the hill past crumbling Victorian summer houses. Then we were among fields and small villages for a time, then a harbour lined with houseboats, elaborate affairs with balconies and patio windows – one had an entire bungalow built on the deck. They were settling gently into their mud berths as the tide fell. There were dismasted dinghies floating outside a clubhouse. Across the water they are closing the huge doors on a boatyard shed. A haze like smoke blurred the outlines of things. The shore blended into the sea and shaded into the scrub trees of the roadside. England looked different down here. London felt like another world, or at least another country.

I asked her about this island, what was its character, how was it different or the same as the old island we used to call home before death came to us on the shore. Predictably she talked about the stones. Chalk, apparently, chalk downs, chalky limestone and marl, fossils, London clay.

I told her about our mother, although she didn't ask.

We had to stop on a causeway with the harbour on one side and a bog on the other. I could see she was impatient. A lorry and a tractor were manoeuvring to pass each other. I had time to see that this was a tamer sea, the harbour shallow. The distant bleak gleam of mudflats stretched towards the English Channel. There was something closed about the sky. A sullen god lurked in its coverts.

She gets agitated, I said, you remember she used to be like that even before. Remember how she worried about having food in the house that we could use if we got cut off in a storm? She worries about her pills all the time now. She's always double-checking that she's taken them. Sometimes she empties them out on the table and counts what's left and divides it by the number of days since the last prescription. She fusses about small things. It turns to efficiency at work, but at home it's a bit strange – you know, strange.

Jeannie didn't seem to be listening.

She's still beautiful, that's the amazing thing. I mean, people who don't know her are always impressed. Her eyes are on fire. I'd like her to find a new man, but I don't think she will.

Look at that tractor, Jeannie said, he shouldn't be coming this way.

Jeannie, I said, Mam worries about you.

She put her hand to the horn but didn't blow.

You'll like Maggie, she said. She's your kind of person. She reminds me of you.

Quite deliberately I choose to say: I think she'll commit suicide one day, I think so anyway.

She stares at me. Who are you talking about?

Your mother, I say, and mine. Remember her?

Seven

I travel from a jagged uplift in what is otherwise water, call it an island, to this other island, a shelf of chalk born of the slow settling out of minerals from a subtropical sea. How did I feel about that? I am too young to remember. Grace remembers everything. She remembers that I cried the day I left and that I wanted my mother. But my mother went somewhere else. I do not remember that. But I remember the feeling that the hardship was over, that things would be warmer, drier and more comfortable now and there would be hot water. It is a betrayal I suppose, but children cannot help betraying people.

Above all I am with my father.

Jeannie, he says to me one day, quite casually, Jeannie, I've found someone else, her name is Maggie, I think you'll like her. They are the magic words. They mean permanence. Now I know the Atlantic is over, the storms, the rain, the cold. I smile at him and he relaxes. Did I, as a child, detect his fear? I put my hand in his and I feel its hugeness, its warmth. Then we move. I don't know where we were or where we were going, but I remember that after he told me and I put my hand in his hand we walked somewhere. The feeling of that movement is still with me. Tom and I, holding hands, moving towards or away from something. I was ten, I think.

How do I adapt to a country where understatement is a form of exaggeration? Here where people are asked not to park their cars near the church and don't, where a sign saying *There is no right of way across this land* is believed. I fit in because I'm a child and a child's life is a parallel universe, or more accurately a set of equiprobable states. Time is a child playing with dice in the morning, love played my life away. But I remember terrors. What do I say to people? I remember Tom playing Grace's games. If you're nice to Maggie, I'll take you swimming. If you behave yourself at so-and-so's house I'll bring you to see the pirate cave. Even little girls like pirates. And there were slaps and punishments. I climbed a tree in someone's garden and mocked her son who was afraid to climb it. Tom took my pants down and smacked me hard. They did it in those days. I broke into a neighbour's shed and fed the finches. That time I was shut in my room for a day and made to apologise. Another time I had an itch between my legs and I scratched it and Maggie, she was there by then, slapped my hand and called it dirty. I laughed at her and she slapped my face and that made me laugh again. She was furious. I don't remember the punishment for scratching my fanny in public but it was terrible enough that I never did it again.

Nevertheless, I am happy. I am part of a normal family. We do not grow our own vegetables and fail at it. We do not go shopping in a leaking boat. We go shopping in a Hillman Avenger or sometimes in Maggie's Anglia. Two cars. Not many families have two.

I fall in love with the garden, our crocuses, our plum trees, our raspberry canes, our peonies, our Lenten Roses. In the Spring finches strip the buds, little brutal bandits, and jays come in July and eat the plums. Tom says they have to live too and there's enough for everyone. Slugs make holes in the strawberries and something else eats the apples. Tom says, Let them be, they live here too. We forage as best we can between their riots. There are striped deck chairs and Victorian seats with cast-iron frames. There's a gravel path that comes from the seabed of the channel, mainly Quaternary chert with an iron oxide coating. I'm fascinated by the bright yellowed pith around the dark heart.

I suppose Tom can afford it, this otherworld of post-Victorian perfection. The best-selling author of *Living an Island, Loving the World*, *The Death of Perfection* and *Falling in Love With A Stone*.

He and I walk the bridle ways together and discover the bee orchid, calamint and columbine. On the beaches we find fossils buried in the cliff face, old stone bones buried a hundred and fifty million years ago and sliced out of the chalk by last night's gale. He designs our walks so that the island will slowly reveal itself. I remember walking along the tide line at low water and finding the fossilised footprints of an iguanodon. I remember staring at the footprint and staring at Tom. Did he bring me here deliberately? Did he already know about this? Or had I just stumbled on something? I remember him squatting on his haunches and dusting the sand off. Me too, our hands touching, our heads close. I wonder, he says, staring at the track of toe-prints that seem almost to contain the noise of the huge beast's passing, I wonder if we might find fossils around here. He didn't know! My heart hammering in my chest. A discovery, an actual discovery! An hour's poking in the cliff produces a stone vertebra. I believe we have simply stumbled upon it. A week later he brings me a book. The island is famous for its fossils. It's the chalk. Of course, he chose the time and the place and the state of the tide. Thus he makes a scientist of me by magic and wishful thinking and subterfuge. That, in a way, is how science is. This is the iguanodon's story: it walked this track, it left its footprints in the mud and later it died and its bones were covered in a fine powder of chalk. We know so little about the iguanodon because there is no perspective that can bring us the light of the evening, the texture of his skin, the colour of his eyes, his reaction to our presence. What we know is a guess, an act of faith in these bones, these prints, this chalk. As it is for science, so it is for human relations also. We exist together in faith and trust. Or their opposites. The slow deposition of meaning that is a life lived, a tale told, depends entirely for its truth on our closeness, our point of view, our willingness to follow the track and the extent to which our very presence alters the situation. Easily we become intruders in our own story.

Eight

My father's second wife was ten years older than me. I can't say I liked her but I suppose I thought her temporary and scarcely worth bothering with. She was cool but not cold. I could see she was anxious to befriend me. She must have known what was happening to my mother. She was an attractive woman in that clear blank bourgeois way. I think she wanted me to feel at home, or perhaps she thought she needed to make me love her. Second wives do.

She told me, with a perfectly serious face, that my father was in John F. Kennedy Airport; his flight had been cancelled and he was waiting for the next free seat. He was very anxious to see me. He had telephoned just before I arrived. He was on a speaking tour. It was very lucrative. They needed the money because the mortgage was frightful.

I knew what my face was doing. I was proud of myself that I held the tears back. Jeannie was watching me and I thought I saw that she was triumphant, or at least pleased. She had composed her face into a sympathetic frown. I wanted to hit her.

84

He so wanted to see you, Maggie said.

My mother…, I said.

But Maggie cut me off. Did I like Italian food? She had given me a room overlooking the garden. Jeannie would be next door. The bathroom was upstairs and a loo down. She was sure I would like to freshen up. Did I need anything?

She hurried me along, pointing at the loo, leading me upstairs, pointing at the garden, Jeannie's room, the bathroom.

Listening carefully, head tilted towards the bedroom window, I could hear the sea. The sound was long-range, arriving on a flat trajectory from somewhere in the past. The room was badly proportioned. The ceiling was too low, the windows too small, the walls too thick. The floor sloped in two directions; I felt giddy looking down. But there was a shower in the bathroom. I hadn't had one since boarding school. In the Kingsland flat we had a cast-iron bath. For dinner Maggie served steak with Heinz spaghetti in tomato sauce. And afterwards there was ice cream and fresh raspberries from the garden.

It was a big rambling house with a long narrow garden that led down to a small copse of elm and some kind of field or park where people walked in the evenings and young people played ball. There were French windows, I remember, and a stagnant almost empty pond. They used to have fish, she said, but the herons got them. There were striped deck chairs on the dead lawn. It was the hottest summer in England since records began.

They held a party for me that first night, and their friends invested the house and spilled out into the garden. They drank wine and gin and tonic and Teacher's whiskey. There were small things to eat. No one seemed to bother that my father was in New York.

Except me.

I knew what he was doing. He didn't want to see me. He never did. Neither me nor my mother. We were over and done with.

Rejection.

Oh Electra, who desires her father because she can't have her mother in her father's place. All that Freudian shit. The simple truth was he was never there. He abandoned me and he abandoned her. He was never there, in fact, to abandon us, but he might have saved us. Saved her. He might just have visited her in that place, that house of hurt and shame. He might have, just once, taken his responsibilities upon himself.

My father. My absent father. My father hunger.

I discovered, to my surprise, that he had a collection of Beatles records and some bootleg tapes. This was revealed to me by a young man who turned out to be a television producer. We went into the drawing room. The records were arranged in chronological order so we began with *Please Please Me*. It was an expensive Pye hi-fi. His name was Bill Langley and he was impressed by the sound quality. He was a very good dancer. People came and went and others danced too. My sister Jeannie came to watch. The song told us that we were just seventeen and we knew what it meant, and he couldn't imagine himself dancing with anyone else once he had seen me standing there. And as we twirled and twisted to each other, in the heat of the evening and stifling room, it could almost seem to be true.

We played everything as far as *Revolver*. One of Bill Langley's gifts was that he could do a perfect twist.

So where do you live, he said.

With my mother in London.

He worked for Granada, he said. Had I seen *A Family At War*?

I was drunk by then.

I said I was born into one.

He laughed too loudly.

He said, Jolly good. Until then I hadn't realised that people still said 'jolly'. I had never heard it said in the East End, nor in my college. It seemed to belong to a different England.

I kissed him at the gate when he was leaving. My heels sank in the gravel. It wasn't my first kiss, but it was my first deliberate one, at a time and place of my choosing. It felt better for that. His cheek to mine. Em loved to rest her cheek against mine when I had been swimming. Her warm face against my cold. Sometimes parts of me ached with loss. Physical hollows where flesh had been. Phantom limbs. Her legs twined around mine in the sand. Tell me a story Gracey.

Beyond the gate there was a little village green and a churchyard, and a parish house and a public library. The lights on the fish and chip shop flickered. There was a moon over the dying elms. The gravestones gleamed silver and bronze; I could see them over his shoulder. He wore Old Spice. His cheeks were like a girl's. He would be around for another ten days, he said, then it was back to the mill. Someone was in the shadows by the garage. We heard their murmured conversation. It's the Irish girl and Bill Langley. Yes, I thought so. It's nice they hit it off.

They must have thought that kissing makes you deaf.

He drove off towards the country. He said he would take the long way round in case PC Plod was on his rounds. Some friends had their names taken the night before. He imitated PC Plod. What 'ave we got 'ere then? I must warn you that anyfink you say may be taken down and given in evidence. It didn't sound like an accent that was ever spoken anywhere, a lucky dip of whatever Bill thought was rustic enough. He said he would pick me up tomorrow. There was another party somewhere. There was always a party in the summertime. It was a party island.

Next morning conversation was difficult. I could not see why. Had I broken a rule by kissing Bill Langley? Jeannie wouldn't even look at me. Tea or coffee Grace? The acrid smell of Nescafé. She mixed it with milk and sugar first, then poured the boiling water. Toast? Thanks. Marmalade? Yes please. Silence.

Thank you for the party.

It was jolly good fun, wasn't it.

Jeannie looked as if a bee had stung her.

Yes, I said, hesitatingly, I really enjoyed myself.

So I saw, Maggie said. She smiled. I smiled. Jeannie looked away.

Jeannie had a crush on Bill. I could see it now. She probably had a crush on everybody. She was that age.

I'll let you two girls get on with it then, Maggie said. Call if you need anything, I shall be in the drawing room.

Jeannie and I sat in the kitchen in the sunlight drinking our instant and eating buttery toast with marmalade from a stoneware jar that said Frank Cooper's 'Oxford'. Maggie sat in the next room listening to BBC Four. We must have talked about something because I remember the news and then *Woman's Hour*, which came on around midday. After that she came in and sat with us. More Nescafé.

I asked what my father was doing in America.

He was trying to move into travel writing, she said. It was a natural development, and he was convinced that travel was the future. He was writing a book about Ireland to begin with. There was talk of a television series – Bill was interested in making it. He had been in touch with his contacts. She was very excited. It was almost finished after three years work! Imagine! When Richard came down they were going to discuss it. Richard knew people, of course, he had contacts in the publishing world. Richard was quite well-known for a poet.

I could see that she would be excited. It was an exciting life.

I thought he was mainly trying to stay away from me but I held my tongue. Instead I said Marvellous. It was a word I never used. We did not say words like that at university. My mother never said it. But last night at the party I heard it many times; the weather was marvellous; the start of Cowes Week was marvellous and Prince Philip was marvellous because he was there.

Marvellous, I said. I protected myself with irony. There was a cold centre in me that was anaesthetic in its usefulness. But it hurt too, as I moved, like shrapnel in my gut. She didn't notice.

She asked me about my studies. She wasn't very interested and I formed the impression that the academic life meant failure to her. It did not compare with the acting and doing of a life in business, which was how she viewed my father's activities. I seem to remember that she used the word boffin. You'll be a boffin. Although I may have invented that. I think she thought of the life of the mind as a form of cowardice.

But at least, she said, you can go into practice. I believe there's a fortune to be made. I see you in Harley Street eventually. Wouldn't that be fun? Or you could go to America. They're always running to head doctors.

Yes, Jeannie said glancing up eagerly, you could go to America.

And later Jeannie and I walked a bridle path that led along the backs of gardens and through a beech wood. It was Beatrix Potter and Jane Austen and all the clichés between. We came to a beach. Jeannie said the stones were chalk flints, Tertiary flints and quartz pebbles, all rolled round by the sea a million years ago. But there were also fragments of ironstone, sarsenstone, lydianstone, hornstone. She made them sound like a poem in some unknown language. I saw that she loved stones in a way that she could never love anything else. Until now I had only known London. London was England for me and my island was far away on the edge of the known world. Beyond the edge, because time erased its features stone by stone. My London wilderness was London Fields or maybe Highgate Cemetery, one of mother's favourites. She used to go and sit on the marble plinth and lean her back against Karl Marx's monument. Workers Of All Lands Unite. She used to tell me stories about Karl Marx on the piss, breaking street-lamps on Tottenham Court Road and running from the police. She liked that sort of thing. She was a romantic. I preferred Abney Park where the founder of the Salvation Army was buried. Abney Park was really a wilderness then.

Jeannie held my hand. There was something childlike about her. I don't know what occasioned this change. Perhaps she regretted her surliness of the morning, perhaps she was moody. I was glad of the warmth. Her hand was small but her fingers were hard and strong.

Daddy liked his home comforts, Jeannie said suddenly. She meant that was why he married again. It was in answer to an unasked question. But probably we both wondered about it.

Then there was a flood of questions. She said she missed me. Did I ever think of home? Of the island? She wondered if the old house was safe. What had become of our little boat? Had the mice taken over? Had the watchtower fallen into the sea?

She let go of my hand. Then she caught it again. She squeezed. She had long fingernails. They gleamed, a black lacquer like the polish on a Chinese box. A column of gleaming beetles folded onto the back of my hand.

Suddenly, I felt cold. I remembered a precise image. My mother sitting restless in the old scrofulous lady-chair in the absolute stillness after a storm, the whole island waiting. Her feet were tapping, her right hand scratching her left hand, blinking rapidly, licking her lips, as restless as a wren. It was after Em died. I had forgotten. I saw in my mind's eye that her nails were bitten to the quick.

Do you ever think about Em, I said.

Jeannie looked sideways at where the sea was evacuating the long groins of the beach. It made her look furtive.

Don't blame yourself, she said. That's what Daddy says.

Do you remember that day?

No, she said. Never.

She used to have bad dreams. She used to come into my bed.

She was Richard's pet, Jeannie said. Jane was against her. Remember she was always saying that Em was her accident.

92

No, I said. She was Jane's favourite. You were Richard's favourite.

No, she said, it was Em.

I'm not sure what I remember, I said. I think I make things up.

She was always talking even when there was no one there, Jeannie said. I heard her. I said Stop talking to yourself. She looked at me. She had my bones. She was hiding them. I caught her by the hand. I pulled her. I'm talking about Em now. I pulled her away and she fell. It was as simple as that. She fell and she scraped her knee and I got into trouble for it because it was my day to mind her. Richard was angry about it. Em could wind Richard around her little finger.

What are you talking about Jeannie, she was just a baby.

Some day ... I can't remember. She was always stealing things. She was a nosy parker. Jane was always angry about her. She was always going off on her own.

What are you saying? Jesus Jeannie!

I blame Mother. She had no self-control. Children need limits. They need to know where they are.

We stared at each other. Her eyes were bright. Her fists were clenched. She was like someone who had struck a blow and was waiting for the response. I took a deep breath.

Is that what Daddy says?

She flared at me, her face livid, her eyes bright.

You hate him!

No, I said, no.

Yes, you hate him. And I love him and I won't let you harm him.

I thought she would attack me, hit me, tear my eyes out. I even saw her extend her fingers with those beetle-black nails. Then she turned away just as suddenly. She walked further along the beach stooping under a flayed elm-tree with its roots in the air, its head in the tide. She stopped on the other side.

This is my favourite place, she said. Nobody comes here. I sit in that tree and watch the ships.

She was talking to me over the unseemly under-things of the tree. Her eyes were dead again. There was only a dab of red on each cheek to memorialise her fury. I calmed myself deliberately.

Jeannie, I said, what is it like living with Daddy?

I saw her nostrils flaring like an animal. She was daring me, it seemed. To what?

Then she said: He takes care of me. Daddy is the caring type. Em would never have died if Daddy had been there.

Don't say that.

No, no, I'm wrong. The watchtower was dangerous. If she climbed up on the wall ... *If* she climbed up on it.

She fell from the tower.

She was angry again. Her eyes gleamed dark as her nails.

I don't remember that.

The coroner's court...

I just put it out of my mind. It's as simple as that. There's no use remembering. Daddy says not to go over things. Think of the present, he says. Concentrate on what's happening around you.

She looked around.

The raised beach is still here, she said. It's under the turf. It runs all along this side.

She pointed at a line of shells and gravel.

There's a shell midden, she said. Iron age I think.

What does he say about me? Daddy.

He says you're the brilliant one. You'll go far. He says no one ever knows what's going on inside your head. You're the genius and I'm the beauty and Em was our special sister. Maggie says she's with the angels. I didn't think Protestants believed in angels. She's probably saying it because she thinks I do. And I don't. Would you give me a hug?

She moved towards me.

Please, she said.

I put my arms around her. I did it badly, I know. I was awkward, unpractised at affection. I realised that I didn't understand her. Already she was taller than me. My head was against her breast. She put her arms around my shoulders and I put mine around her waist. The long-legged fly and the stone. I don't know how long we stayed like that. Did we glisten like enamel, mica, oil? From a ship in the channel we must have looked permanent, a realist sculpture on the shore, depicting loss, disaster, exile. A mother and child. A sailor and his lass. But it would have been a lie. After a time she patted me on the head as you would pat a child. We're still sisters, she said. Then she stepped away and turned her back on me.

Nine

Daddy encouraged her geology and mineralogy, she said. I tried that the other way round. Daddy encouraged my psychology. It didn't work. I was jealous, I knew that. I was not a fool. He brought her books. When he was travelling he always thought of her. She was allowed to search his bags. She was allowed to find things. Sometimes he brought stones. She had a piece of alabaster from Italy, a banded agate from Greece and a moss agate from America. He hides things from me, she said. I found the alabaster in the lining of his old leather bag. It's a game we play.

She had one stone that she didn't keep with the others. She had a small velvet-covered box in her pocket, a jewel-box, but she wore no jewellery. She must have brought it specially to show me. She opened it. There was a cushion of velvet and a piece of limestone with a ring of faded yellow lichen. It was triangular in shape, almost like an arrowhead. It looked strange and savage. It didn't belong here. She watched me.

This is private, she said. It's not part of the collection. What does it mean?

The lichen is dead of course. I used fixative. I was afraid it would turn into dust.

Is it from home?

It's from the tower. It reminds me.

She laughed nervously. She held the box on her palm, her fingers curled around it. I noticed her hand was shaking slightly. She did not offer it to me to hold.

Funny isn't it, she said. I never show it to anybody. It's letting Daddy down I think. I'm not allowed to mention the island. No sad thoughts, he says. Unhappy memories are unsanitary. There's no going back he says. I have to let go. Sometimes Richard wants to talk about it and Daddy gets angry. I hate it when he gets angry.

Does Richard come down here?

Of course he does.

What does he look like now? We haven't seen him in London for four years.

The same. He looks like he always did. That's a funny question.

I forget really. I forget what he's like. I don't remember the details.

Well, Jeannie said, he's tall and thin. Fair hair. Blue eyes. I don't remember really.

His eyes are green. A kind of grey-green, like mine.

You know more about it than I do.

It's grand, I said, it doesn't matter.

She put the stone back in the ring box. She put the box in her pocket again.

98

You know Jeannie, I said, sometimes I think, what about if we could have stopped it? I mean, should we have been taking care of her? I mean, we didn't mean to do anything. What I mean is, did we do it?

What are you talking about?

What they said at the coroner's. I'm talking about Em. Can you remember what happened that day. Can you remember anything?

I told you. We have to move on. That's what Tom says.

She climbed up on the tree. She hooked her leg under one of the branches and leaned backwards so far she almost seemed to be leaning out of the world. She said hanging upside down was a cure for fear of heights. Because it feels like you're looking up. The tide was coming in. I heard it filling between the stones. Don't lean too far back Jeannie, I said. You'll fall.

I was conscious of a desire for something to happen. Something to shake things. If she fell what would I do?

She straightened up suddenly.

I never fall, she said.

She sprang down.

Swim, she said. You can bring me back a sea-man. Do you remember? She used to tell us stories? I was always frightened. Take your clothes off. Daddy says you're brazen. The sea is where you belong.

I swam out into the channel. I was conscious that the water was not very deep. At one point, a long way out, my feet touched mud. At the equinoctial springs, I had read, people walked off the island as far as a mud bank and played a game of cricket there. It was a tradition. It was important that they never got their feet wet. I imagined the mud gleaming in the autumn sun, the people in white walking where now I was swimming.

Out there I got a better idea of the island. There was a low wooded shore. There were homes among the trees, many of which had slipways and boathouses, Victorian or Edwardian seaside architecture with overhanging eaves, decorative spindles and gingerbread trim. To the west they ran towards a long wooden pier, to the east they disappeared into woods. There was the long sweep of sand at the harbour entrance. On the outer side some bathing huts and caravans, a stone belfry that had no church. The stones that sailors used to scour the decks of the old ships came from here. It's name was Holystone. So Jeannie said.

I swam back. Jeannie was waiting. She watched me coming ashore. I changed under the towel.

Jeannie, I said, where is Em buried?

What? I don't know.

Mother asked me. She doesn't know.

I don't know.

We walked back to the house and when we got there we heard the news that my father would be staying in America for at least an extra week. He had been asked to write something for the *Observer* about the American Bicentennial celebrations. His second wife thought it was exciting. I thought he was probably sleeping with someone. And I thought he was afraid of me. He was afraid of my memories anyway. Jeannie went away someplace without saying anything. I decided to leave the following day.

Alone in the house later that afternoon I lay on the bed in my underclothes with the windows open, my mind twisting and turning. Guilt is like a never-healing wound. Once I dozed and woke to the sensation of Em's nose in my back, her breath moistening between my shoulder blades. I had been dreaming my usual dream. I saw her fall. In my dreams I am looking up, my arms outstretched. Em, come down to me, jump. And she jumps. But there's always something wrong. I can never reach out far enough to catch her.

Outside there were sparrows in distress. They stood in the shade with their wings lifted, trying to stay cool. They were silent. The island was silent. People who could, stayed indoors. It was the hottest year since records began. England was burning. Coming down in the train I had seen the smoke of the New Forest. We could see it now from the island. They wanted people to put bricks in the toilet cisterns to save water. Hurn Forest burned – or perhaps that was later. And perhaps later too, because these things are always too late, they appointed a Minister for Drought.

I got up about four and opened the bedroom door. It swung back and came to a stop, halted by a rise in the floor. Over the years, I saw, a swooping channel had been followed by that swing and the lower corner of the door was softened and rounded. Objects accommodate themselves because they have no consciousness. I tiptoed along the creaking landing and stopped at Jeannie's door. I knew she was out but still I tested the handle. It opened noiselessly.

The room was bare except for a bed, a chair, a desk. There were no pin-ups or photographs. She had a patchwork quilt. In her wardrobe there were hiking boots and a canvas knapsack. There were stones on her windowsill – I recognised some that she had named to me that morning – and several tiny fossilised shells in an Andrews Liver Salts tin, and a small but perfect stone sea urchin, a slightly irregular dome with five dotted stripes that met at the crown. The piece of paper it stood on said *heart-urchin, echinoderm, poss. cretaceous*. It looked like it was made of mud but it felt comfortable in the hand, a hundred million years for the living creature to set into stone. Down on the scrap of lawn a bullfinch sorted through tissue-thin leaves. His hard black head moved in increments like a clockwork toy.

She had Rachel Carson's books. To Jeannie, with love Daddy. The bookseller was in New York. And she had *A Geological History Of The British Isles* and *Structure Of The British Isles* and the local section of *British Regional Geology*. It was the beginnings of a collection.

She had a diary. I opened it at random. It was the usual teenage angst. She had a crush on someone called B. There were breathy, Mills & Boonish accounts of meeting him at the newsagents. *I saw his ramrod straight back before me. His head held high. The warmth of his smile.* Notes about stones, about indigestion, about the temperature in the shade. The detail is there, the determination to be scientific. The hot weather. I flicked through the week's entries. She did not mention me. Perhaps she would get round to it in retrospect, when I was gone. G came down for few days. Got on well. Had fun. Doesn't smoke. Went back to London.

Banalities.

The master bedroom was sweet with scent. A translucent peignoir on a hanger hooked to the door of the wardrobe. A nylon négligée thrown on the bed, the bed itself unmade. Scent bottles and a powder box and a glass tray with a spike for holding rings. There were no rings on it. Gold lamé slippers on a goatskin rug. A paperback of Arthur Hailey's *Airport* open and face down. A packet of Anadin. Sex and scent and analgesics. I could easily have been overcome by it, overwhelmed, the thoughts of bodies and sweat and transparent nightclothes.

The next room was my father's office. I thought it would be his bedroom. There was a large locked filing cabinet. A clock that told the time in New York, London and Tokyo. A mahogany bookcase that mostly contained his own books in different editions and languages. The centre of the room was taken up by a partner's desk with a chair at both sides. On its vast gleaming surface there was a Remington typewriter and a block of blank paper; opposite them, in front of the second chair, a typescript. I listened for any sounds in the house or garden but there were none.

He was writing about my mother. I think my mother's appearances in his books represented for her absolute truths about her life and personality. They came swift as judgement and struck her to the bone. This other self that we never express. They were first of all ideal forms of her life, potential existences that she always failed to realise. They were myths of happiness and self-sufficiency. Then there were tales of her madness fixed forever in words not of her choosing. They were his narrative of how she fell from grace; her lapses, her comical aporia, her diatonic weeping, her infidelity. She saw herself. She understood that she was an ex-angel, a pitiful fallen creature with a broken wing. She saw too that he was her imprisoned narrator. His readers would long for his release. Now he was beginning again. The starting point was different. This was memoir.

Not many people know that potatoes and tomatoes belong to the same family, *Solanaceae*, and it's a bit counter-intuitive, considering that they belong at opposite ends of the plants, as it were, the tuber and the fruit. But it's an incontestable truth that potatoes grow well in the soil of an island on the eastern edge of the Atlantic at 51° 30' North, and tomatoes do not. To put this in perspective consider that 51° 30' N on the western side of the Atlantic is Newfoundland and the Strait of Belle Isle which is iced up for ten months of the year. Nevertheless, and despite my advice, Jane persisted in her belief that the children should have tomatoes in summertime to eat with their salads. To achieve this impossible task she set about buying a glass house in bits and pieces, an old wooden glasshouse that was once attached to the southern wall of a Victorian cottage about twenty miles away on the mainland. She had it imported to our island, panel by panel, on the post boat which could spare the time in winter to call at our pier but which was too busy in the summer. Eugene O'Driscoll the boatman couldn't understand it. I remember him scratching his forehead with his cap held back and saying, 'Jasus now, Tom, divil a glasshouse there was on the islands until today. Sure if it was going to work wouldn't you think the gentry would have tried it before now.' When she had it all unbroken leaning against our gable she began to give thought to how to assemble it. She began to make trips ashore for brass screws and various tools. She ordered cement in bags and red bricks to be delivered to the pier. But she never got around to doing any of it and that was how we ended up with fossilised cement bags that had been soaked in April rain, a million self-tapping screws and stacks of glassy window-frames. Luckily the bricks never arrived. But every now and then we would all parade around to the gable end and contemplate the jigsaw of the glasshouse and make elaborate plans for putting it all together on some fine calm summer's day. She loved glass and often brought a kitchen chair out to contemplate the setting sun as reflected in the greening surfaces. At the very least, she claimed, the glass insulated and warmed the gable which was always the coldest wall in the house because it was turned towards the prevailing wind. It was, I think now, an irrational thing, an obsession. It was an early warning that I didn't heed.

I didn't remember any glasshouse.

There was a full account of how we came out of the island. How the men on the lifeboat turned their backs out of natural sympathy. One of them was the fisherman who called to tell his stories and who came and went that night that we heard her screaming. He never looked at any of us. It was a wet day. They wore their long sou'westers, their sea-boots. They were rough men. They made their living by farming or fishing but they volunteered to save people. They had seen madness before; the hills and the valleys were full of it. They did not want their eyes to say what they saw. They watched the sea and the boat and tended to it with skill and gentleness while my mother wept and raved and my father held her together and we children could not close our eyes. In a sense they had always known this would happen. They had seen her coming ashore on her foraging trips, seen the things she bought, heard her talk. They knew about her wild life in the wilderness of the Atlantic where no woman in her right mind would want to live – in remote places everybody knows everything, or they think of it that way. They saw the kind of children she reared. There's a want there – that was a phrase she picked and brought with her – meaning she was not the full shilling, she'd heard it used. Maybe it was intended for her.

Where was Flanagan the cat? Cats can look after themselves and I suppose we always intended to go back for him, but none us ever did.

And there the chapter ended. Chapter two was entitled 'The Mental: Cork'. Now I saw that what he had done was turn it into a story and the story had made everything that happened inevitable and that inevitability absolved us all, but most of all, him. What I wanted most of all was to burn it. What I did was arrange the paper carefully so no one would know. I left the room and closed the door. I could see why he had taken so many years to write it. It would be a difficult book.

I went up on the downs. I needed to walk and think. High up on the island's back there were larks rising and cowbells, and people following the bridle paths, a seemingly natural arrangement of clichés and stereotypes. Over the village the evening picked out the green oxide of the Methodist church, giving it a kind of subterranean pallor as though the saved had somehow lifted the veil to draw a little vigour in. I tried to think about my father.

About whether truth was necessary as everybody said, or whether one could live better by illusion. How much revelation was necessary or desirable? All things that are, are lights. I came to no conclusions, of course, despite my training. Freud once said that psychology would only be completely possible in a society that no longer needed it.

It was a kind of pain, a kind of loss, as though I had been given the wrong life.

Bill Langley picked me up at eight and he drove me across the downs again to a pub where some friends of his were meeting. I remember the names, magical to me, like a story by Thomas Hardy: Culver Down, Yaverland, Nunwell, Morton, Whippingham. He had a new Ford Escort. I drank bitter and Bill drank gin. Then he drove me to a house. There was a keg of beer and a man from the Village Inn to pour it. There were lights in the trees and there was a small jazz band. I never heard what the party was about. It may have been a birthday or an engagement or a wedding, although the bride and groom must have been long gone by the time we got there. People said frightfully and horrid and jolly. We were called the young people, and in return Bill called them the Enid Blytons. Allowances were made for us. When we danced nobody minded. The Enid Blytons went indoors early and left the world to us. We heard their laughter in the silences between sets. We danced in the light of the trees until the band put their instruments down. We made our goodbyes. Cheerio Grace, Cheerio old chap, you know what they say, try to keep it in your trousers. He drove me home. In the swinging car, reeling up over the Downs, in the dreamy watery light of Bill's headlamps, somewhere between The Hare & Hounds and home I recognised the only thing that would ever fix my life – revenge. It was a game I could play. The thought made me light-headed.

There was kissing in his car outside the public library. I could see the light in Jeannie's room. There was some fumbling and touching but not very much. It was too hot. He drove off towards the windmill, going the long way round. I had not told him I was returning to London in the morning.

My sister Jeannie said she would like to come up to London sometime to see our mother. Maggie thought it was a wonderful idea. It seems she had been taking advice about stepmothers. She said that it would be good for Jeannie to stay in contact. She wanted to make arrangements there and then. She took a calendar down from the kitchen wall and started counting weeks and asking whether weekdays or weekends would be most convenient. Woodfull Butchers First-Class Meat, the calendar said. I said that I would need to ask mother. She wasn't always able for visitors. She had her bad days. The thing is, it was difficult to say in advance. She could be funny about things.

Suddenly Maggie understood. I saw it appearing in her eyes like a flaw of wind on a flat sea. I was grateful for it. She did not press me about Jeannie coming up.

You go on and see how things are, she said, and let us know when it suits. Don't you worry about a thing dear.

Jeannie caught the tone.

Oh, she said. She didn't look at us.

Then she said, She's my mother too.

What shall I tell Bill Langley if he comes? Maggie said.

Tell him anything you like.

Shall I give him your telephone?

I shrugged. Jeannie looked big cow's eyes at me.

The thought came to me: You can have him if you take mother. But I didn't say it.

Before I left I slipped into the office and took the typescript. I replaced it with the same thickness of blank paper from the block. I put it in my vanity bag. There was no bin at Portsmouth Pier so I held onto it until Waterloo. Jeannie drove me to the boat. I remember when she was a little girl she had a book called *Aurora The Sleeping Beauty*, it was a colouring book based on the Walt Disney Motion Picture. And in it Princess Aurora became Briar Rose. I remember her sitting in the window colouring the outlines. There is always something extra in the light of an island. It is the presence of the sea, like living in a world where there is always a mirror just out of sight.

My mother's horror was terrible. I remember very little of it. There was a time when I recalled it all but I found it useless in dealing with her life or my

110

own. Memory is an overrated capacity. It is most useful to those who need to deny things. I remember she was upstairs in bed and my sister Jeannie and I were sitting in the kitchen and Em was dead. There were night lights on the table because the electricity cable had failed, as it often did – boats were forever anchoring on it, despite the warning signs. My father and Richard Wood were upstairs. We could hear my mother's voice. It came in rapid stuttering bursts, like a sewing machine. I remember that an earwig walked across the table in front of us. Jeannie pinched it up and held it to the light. I saw its jaws working, its tail bending and straightening, its antennae. Then she dropped it into the night light. It fell into the molten wax and settled quickly down. It drowned. In the morning there was the shadow of the earwig in the cold wax.

My mother's horror was also perfectly reasonable. One of the things we forget is that the world itself is madder than anything our heads can make. How should one remember one's child falling into the sea? Sustaining injuries against the cliff on the way down? After that everything is impossible.

My mother's horror was all-encompassing, all-consuming. It devoured the night and the day, the sun and the moon, God and the future and everything in between. It paralysed us. It divided us.

Jeannie was crying too. I resented her for doing it. It seemed to me she wanted as always to be the centre of attention but nobody paid her any heed. Her tearfulness turned into wailing and then I wanted to choke her. I slapped her once but it only made her worse. Shut up, I said, it's bad enough. Then I said, A pity it wasn't you.

Later, the night before we came out of the island – how long was it between Em's death and our crossing? – I woke to hear running and urgent voices. I stood on the bed to see out the window but I could not see the ground. I ran down and saw that the front door was open. Richard had been sleeping on the kitchen floor. His sleeping bag was empty. I closed the door and went back to bed. My mother's room was empty too. It meant that she had run away again.

After a time I heard the voices coming back. Richard, my father, my mother. They did not go to bed. I fell asleep. In the morning Jeannie said she had been asleep all night but I knew she was not. She was listening too.

Where did my mother go that night? Nobody tells children these things. They hope, maybe they believe, that we sleep through every danger; that childhood is, in fact, a kind of sleepwalk through their adult world. Like someone said that madness is a nightmare in a waking world. And then later they assume we know. As if the simple act of growing up involves absorbing their memories into our own. All that time they were inventing the lie that would ravage my life. I could hear them talking it through. They were talking about me. If I had been older, stronger, wilder I would have run away. I could swim ashore at high tide. It was the kind of thing I was good at. This is what you'll say to the Guards, they told me, and this is what you'll say at the Coroner's Court. And then they told me a lie.

Later I went to see her in the hospital. I was a child. I was lost. My father should have been there but he ran away. Sometimes children find the strength to endure, to sustain the self in the face of the terrible attrition of daily life, but the cost is incalculable. I have seen children for whom the everyday is a nightmare.

They called it The Red Brick and sometimes The Mental. There were old people everywhere. They were doing nothing. My mother was an old person too. She was sitting in a glasshouse with a lot of others. Their chairs were against the wall. They were facing outwards to the winter sun. She did not look out of place. She said nothing for a long time. Then she cried. She called me Child of Grace. It was an old joke of hers. When I heard it I knew she was the same person now as before and I tried to think how I could get her out. I had dreams of organising her escape. Child of Grace, she said, will I tell you a secret? But a nurse came and I never heard the secret. I wasn't sure I wanted to hear it.

When I went to boarding school I was relieved. Because I could do nothing I felt the responsibility was no longer mine. Nothing could be as terrible as watching your mother being mad. But at night I thought about her. I could not stop wondering what it was like to be mad among madwomen, to be in a madhouse, to be hurt, to believe that you had caused the death of your own child, or neglected to save her, to have no way back, to always have that absence, that little nose between your shoulder blades, to be able to feel the steady breathing, or whatever recollection most troubled her, and to know that it was only madness, that the child was dead. The child is dead. There are few worse sentences in the English language.

That was the commonplace book of mother's madness. My father only knew the beginning, but I saw it right through to the end. That obstinate hurt that diverted her life. It made a fanatic of her. It made her immoveable. It made her irretrievably other. She was still my mother. It was impossible. Yeats wrote: Hearts with one purpose alone/ Through summer and winter, seem/ Enchanted to a stone/ To trouble the living stream.

That was her.

Ten

Father came home. Grace went back to London. It is an ordinary evening. I am alone in the kitchen thinking about Bill Langley and other sexual objects while ostensibly looking at the *Radio Times*. From the drawing room I hear canned laughter and Tommy Cooper saying *Just li' that*. In there the heat generated by the TV set is stifling even with all the windows open. When the brassy jazz theme plays Maggie comes out to make tea.

Are you still moping in here, she says. Why don't you go down to the club? You should go out.

I'm reading.

You'll go blind in this light.

She turns on the kitchen light. Almost immediately there are tiny flies on the ceiling, moths drifting through the open window. Nature is frighteningly anxious to come indoors.

Honestly Jean, you'll injure your eyes you know.

What's wrong with Tom? Since he came back he's spent most of his time in his study. He hardly even talks.

Her back is to me. She has spooned the tea in. Now she lifts the kettle and adds boiling water. Her hand is steady. She says nothing.

Maggie? What's wrong with Tom?

Very quietly she says, I don't know.

Then she turns around and takes a packet of cigarettes from the pocket of her skirt. She lights one, sucks deep and exhales. Maggie gave up smoking when she married Tom. He doesn't approve of the tobacco industry.

Tell me what happened between you and Grace.

Nothing. We went for walks. We talked.

Something happened.

Not that I noticed.

Her face is beginning to dissolve. Already what will be the lines of old age are pulling her features apart. Her cheek is slipping. Her eyes are bunching at the edges. Her mouth is inclining downwards. The suck lines that long-term smokers get. There are faint horizontal creases at her neck. She is too young to be growing old. It must be suffering.

She says, I don't understand, Jean.

I don't want to think about it. The world is already too painful. I remember my mother holding a mug of tea a long time ago, it seems, exactly at the cusp of desolation, that night waiting for Tom to come, for the boat to come with the people who would investigate the child's death. Richard was sitting opposite, close to her, his hand on her thigh moving slowly up and down, it was meant to be a comforting movement, how repetition comforts.

116

And over and over again she was saying, I don't know how it happened, I don't understand.

I make up my mind that in the dislocation of Maggie's life and my father's, if it came to that, I would again be on Tom's side. Children are capable of such resolution although we believe they drift from one hapless parent to the next. They have the will to survive.

Whatever it is, I say, it's nothing to do with me. Or Grace.

Never mind, Maggie says, Richard is coming down at the weekend. He always cheers daddy up.

When I think of Richard I always think of hands. Working ropes in the salt and sun, they were hard. The sinews stood out on them. His fingers and palms had calluses. The idea makes me tremble. I have the fever of hot days when everything is sexual.

The day is so hot that there are no birds. Where they went to I don't know. Then suddenly, sometime after six o'clock, there are dozens of swallows. Their thin whistling fills the sky. A pair of white cabbage butterflies almost fly in my window. The sun has gone behind the house and there is shade.

I hear voices in the garden. I bring a lemonade from the kitchen.

Hello Jeannie, Maggie says. She says it brightly but it sounds forced. Have you been working on your collection? Have you seen her collection, Richard?

Richard hasn't.

Oh Jeannie knows all about stones, she says, she's quite the boffin. We wondered where you were dear. I thought you might be at the club.

When Maggie says boffin she means anyone who is a master of useless knowledge. I sense her irritation. I sit down on Richard's side of the table.

His legs are muscular and tanned and the hairs are bleached. There is a fine scar, whiter than the rest of his skin, on the inside of his calf. I ask him about it and he says he caught a fishhook there and the line ran out of his hand suddenly and took the hook with it. Does it hurt still? Not anymore.

I reach out and touch it, briefly, lightly.

Maggie puts her glass down hard.

There's a fine layer of sweat at the lower rim of his shorts. It glistens in the hairs. Maggie is staring at me. Is she afraid? Richard has a half-smile, dreamy and provocative at once. He tilts his glass of Pimms towards me.

You have to watch out for the hooks, he says. They're always going places they shouldn't. And if you're at sea for a few days the cuts'll get infected. The buggers won't heal in the salt.

Jean, would you get some ice, there's a dear, it melts so fast in this heat.

Yes, get some ice Jeannie.

Ice is exactly what we need.

Later. Richard's door is ajar so I go in. He's sitting at his desk with the window open. He puts a finger to his lips. Then he gestures to me to come closer.

Hear that, he whispers, it's a hedgehog.

I listen to the rustling and snuffling and distant grunting. Richard is rapt. I stare at the back of his neck. Moths circle the light, clattering against the paper shade. The wall is peppered with tiny flies. On the paper in front of him I see that he has written a title and three much-revised lines. He has squashed an insect and a tiny black-and-blood stain marked the word 'pig'.

The Hedge Pig Below My Window

The ~~curiously sexual snuffling rutting~~ hedge pig
~~Fills the night beyond my window~~ Snuffles through
the galaxy ~~outside~~
~~Uttering my desire~~ To utter desire below my window

It is the poem that will eventually become 'Hedgehog In The Heatwave', one of his most anthologised shorter poems, apparently a lighthearted description of a hedgehog with his head in a crisp bag, in rhyming quatrains, with a humorous subtext to do with the prickliness of lovers. Lust would disappear from it except for the word 'rutting' and its echo in 'the night's maw uttering'. It would be taught in schools. But for me it will always be about a hot room, unuttered yearning, a night so intense my body runs with sweat, the stark smell of the two of us. That summer.

I keep a diary. Maggie gave it to me, a red leather cover with a brass clasp that fitted into a lock. It had two small brass keys. Hearts were embossed in the leather. When I look at it now I find it astonishing that it contains nothing at all of what was really happening. And perhaps it is all the more intense because its words are really a kind of silence. Are all diaries like that? An earthquake is about to happen, it would leave its mark in the sine wave of our lives, and here is the commonplace book:

Monday: M went to Newport and came back with a blouse for me. I think it makes me look like Anne in *The Onedin Line*. Eeek.

Tuesday: Tom hardly home at all today. Heard him getting his bfast. Then heard his car arrive back about 11 but was already in bed. Found another fossil urchin on the beach. Thought it was a real urchin first. Tried to turn it over, found it was stone. Perfect including both orifices but squashed like a punctured ball.

Wednesday: M bought grapefruit for R. It turned out R didn't eat grapefruit. Comical scene in kitchen. R told story of first person he had ever seen eating gfrt. It was a vicar. Wondered why R was in vicar's house at bfast. Must ask.

Thursday: I hate Bruce Forsyth esp. nice to see you to see you nice. M loves it. Yuk. R goes up to his room to write poetry. He only watches the news.

Friday: Tom asked me if I had taken anything from his study. I said what? He said papers. I said I hadn't been into his study. He said he was missing some papers. I said ask M. Curiouser and curiouser.

Saturday: R agreed to come down to the club. Jane Joy was there but we ignored her. We watched the boats. He likes one type which he calls a scowl or a scow. He bought me a half of beer and warned me not to tell M or F. It was fun. R Says he might come fossil hunting.

There are no entries at all for the following week. The week of the earthquake.

So we are fossil hunting at Undercliff beach. It's a September afternoon after school. The sea is a mirror that stretches as far as the horizon. We've walked miles. He was always one for endurance. He wears Tom's shorts, a pale yellow shirt and a pair of battered rubber dollies. We have a bottle of Robinsons Lemon Barley Water and a butter-paper packet of ham sandwiches.

We sit down to examine our only find, a tiny ammonite from the London Clay, solitary in my canvas bag. Still it is beautiful, coppery, fractured, abstract.

You know, he says, what I love is the imperfections, perfection is a dangerous myth, what we need to love is our immanence not our possibilities.

I know what he means although I don't know what immanence is – it doesn't seem necessary to the thought. Saying immanence means he's treating me as an equal. I like that. I tell him that Grace was asking about him.

She wanted to know if you came down here. She said you never visited Jane. She was very curious about you.

He ignores me. He closes his eyes for a time. When he opens them he indicates the cliffs at our back. Tell me about this place, he says.

So I tell him the story of the chalk and mud that is the island, I know the story well. He lies back, closes his eyes and listens. Even that lying back is accomplished like a deliberate gesture, an unfolding of the body in equilibrium. I have always known this grace. It's part of the landscape of my childhood, as natural as a tree moving in the wind. His body straightens as smoothly as one might open a fist and straighten a hand. His lean face and clear eyes, then the long pale lashes. Now I can look at his face, now that he can't see me. I try to memorise it. The downy hair round his lips, almost like a girl's. In the steely light I see it. And a tiny scar near his left eye, so smooth I feel I could rub it away with my finger.

It's a dream – the flat sea, the hot sand, the canvas bag of tools and the single burnished ammonite. The story of the rock, the clay, the sand, told in millions of years. Sweat on my face, in my armpits, between my breasts and my legs. The humidity is rising. Over on the French side of the channel I can see cumulus building into giant anvils. As I talk I learn something new and it is this: that two people could commit any enormity and it wouldn't alter the long history of stone by as much as a micron. On this day in the four and half billion year existence of the

122

earth I could have exactly what I want, what I had always wanted, and afterwards the universe would be exactly the same without waste, without imbalance. So when I see that he's asleep I bend down and put my mouth close to his. I am careful not to touch. I am so close I can almost feel my own shadow.

He wakes. I draw back. I feel my face redden. I try to look away.

Then he puts his arms around me and pulls me down. Later he says that he did it because he didn't want to hurt me, he didn't want me to feel rejected. But it doesn't feel like that.

First there is the kiss. Everything is rougher than I expected. By the time he feels for my breast I am beyond caring, beyond doing, beyond resistance, beyond common sense. I've fallen for sex, fallen into sex, I'm falling in sex.

He's almost weightless. When he enters me it hurts and my pain belongs to the subterranean world, primitive as the clay. His body is slacker than I expected, a small paunch begins at his waist and settles in a downward parabola to his groin. His pubic hair is red. His erect penis is a surprise although I had imagined what they would feel like, read about them, seen them represented on toilet walls and magazines. I didn't see it before he entered me, but afterwards it is small and sticky and amusing. I want to touch it but I don't dare. I don't know the etiquette. He is twenty or more years older than me. This is sex.

I remember how I ran home carrying the empty bird in the rain and tipped the wet bones out of my sweater onto the table and he made me take my clothes off.

He rolls sideways onto the sand.

Oh god, he says.

I think it sounds like anguish. I don't care. I find I'm holding my breath. I release it slowly. Sex, I tell myself. I've had it. Sex. Somewhere in a disconnected but synchronous life, a point from which I can view myself to advantage and still belong, I am amused. There I am lying in the sand full of semen. This is sex. I've had sex. There are fossils everywhere. I'm marvelling and silently laughing. I'm inwardly celebrating and at the same time reverent. Sex.

I lie there with my legs spread, my shirt pulled down awkwardly. The old bag of tools is beside my head. I can almost sense the numinous reality of the ammonite. I'm sore but not as much as I had imagined. I've been learning things from magazines, though they haven't prepared me for the fullness, the experience of being ridden, of his final explosive stop. The terror is pleasure. There isn't enough of it. I want it again. I want to be able to experience each part of it distinctly not as a single astonishing mass. Sex. It just happened. I've had it.

We talk seriously once we've arranged our clothes again. The clouds have come from France and the sky is lowering. We're at the upper extent of the sand and there are scars of grey clay like the broken crust of the world. First of all there are apologies I don't want. Then there are the people we can't tell. Tom would never speak to him again. As it was, things aren't good between them, he's never seen Tom in such black humour and if he discovered this ... And Maggie would be shocked. She might go to the police. I think the police thing is laughable. And I actually laugh. He doesn't. He is a guest, he has broken the most fundamental rules, if there is a baby he would acknowledge it of course, he would not run away from his responsibilities – all that primitive nonsense. He sits with his knees doubled up under his chin, his arms wrapped around them. He looks like a miserable midget. I want to say to him that this is not 1876, that I know what I'm doing, that I'm not a child, that this is the age of liberation. I've read articles in which people say these things.

I'm so sorry Jeannie, he keeps saying, I'm not good at self control.

In the end, child that I am, I laugh in his face.

Do it to me again, I say as if to prove that I know what I'm doing. I begin to unbutton my shorts.

Oh no, he says, oh no my girl, I'm not falling for it again.

He looks along the beach.

Look, he says, there's a situation, a delicate situation ... once upon a time ...

I know.

He stands up suddenly. He walks towards the water which is coming in our direction. I know this part of the beach can get cut off at spring tide, people have been rescued here. I think about being cut off for six hours or so with Richard. He picks up one piece of shingle after another and launches them into the water. Some skip on the surface for a while before they go down. I watch him. I feel cool and powerful. When he turns round again he stares silently at me for about ten seconds. Then he begins walking back the way we came. When I get up to follow him I feel where he's been. The soreness is a peculiar pleasure, a memento. A child no more, it says.

That evening I take all my clothes off and lie on the bed trembling and sweating. Recollection overwhelms me, a kind of curse, something between desire and fear. An animal pinning me to the sand, his pistoning is like a noise in my head. I try to remember it as it happened step by step. I take a cool shower and walk round the room, backwards and forwards, until the water dries on my skin. I can smell him between my legs. Could other people smell it too? I scrub myself with a coarse cloth Maggie bought in a cosmetics shop; it comes with a special soap and promises to remove the layer of dead skin that dulls the complexion. Each time, after drying, I think the sour-milk smell is still there. Later, months or years later, it would occur to me that the coupling on the beach centred me, a linchpin that held the wheel of my life from spinning away into emptiness and isolation, but that night and for nights afterwards there was only the memory of fullness and the oily functionality of it.

Outside Colonel Souter's dog hunts hedgehogs – I hear their weird metallic craking and the dog's excited yips. Beyond that the island lies in its peaceful sea like an emerald on blue satin. And I dream in words of complex provenance of sex and fucking and penetration and touching – things I've felt, things I've read about, things I project for the future, hopeful pleasures without consequences. Later still I open my secret trove of things belonging to Richard – a button, one of his pencils, a photograph cut from the jacket of one his books, a poem he gave me which I did not understand at the time:

Child

She stands at the very edge of the known
Where falling is pleasure and standing still
Is going back: a breath of wind on her
Trembling skin, or her mother's distant call
In the perfect synchrony of now,
And the fall begins; now she makes her own
Rising gale, the hurry of going down.

For years I thought it was about me. About sex. About surrender. About our illicit copulation, about carnal knowledge.

In the watery heat of an afternoon a few days later we find ourselves alone again. Maggie and Tom have gone out. Maggie cautioned me not to get too much sun. She thought I looked peaky. Heatstroke, she told me solemnly, was something that crept up on one. The wheels on the drive, the gate closing, the car pulling away. Richard is reading Ted Hughes' *Crow*.

When the village is silent again he looks up and says, Well Jeannie?

Well what?

How are you?

I know exactly what he means. I smile. He stands up. I stand up too. For perhaps five seconds we hesitate, paralysed by the possibilities. Then we go upstairs without a word.

He has brought what he calls a johnny – he plans to put it on at the end, just before the climax. He explains this to me carefully. He opens the packet and shows me what will happen. He is delivering a biology lecture about prophylactics – we've had those at school. But in the future its rubbery smell would be the thing that instantly triggers recollection and provokes desire – new cars sometimes had it in those days, beach balls, cheap waterproof coats, rubber gloves. For the first time I hear the ridiculous term *coitus interruptus*. Richard does not believe in it. I tell him I don't care. He says a baby would ruin my life.

So we do it again and he stops at the wrong time to put the johnny on and afterwards there is a ridiculously tiny creamy bubble at the tip. When he did it inside me it felt like a flood, but in the johnny it was a pathetic thing, hardly a stain on a table top.

How long do we have? When Maggie and Tom come back we would hear the car engine running in the silent heat – Tom liked the tick–over set a little too fast – while Maggie opened the gate, the front door opening. Plenty of time for Richard to get into his own bed.

We talk while sweat oils our bodies. We are submerged in desire. Sometimes we become alert enough to hear the distant rumbling of thunder over the mainland. I want everything again and again. I want him to tell me about other women. I want to hear the words. Then, sometime in the haze of the afternoon, I want him to tell me about my parents.

Go away little girl, he says. I won't tell you any secrets.

Richard says he can't continue fucking me in my father's house. We'll get caught, he says. We'll fall asleep and wake up to find the two of them looking down on us.

He has already given me a poem about Hephaestus, the god of craftsmen and fire who was married to Aphrodite and who came home one day to find her in bed with Ares. Hephaestus, who was a blacksmith, it seems, fashioned an invisible net to trap the lovers. When they woke after lovemaking they were unable to leave the bed. He thinks I should like it because Hephaestus is the god of thunder and volcanoes.

I could go on a holiday, I say. You could invite me to Ireland for a few weeks. You could teach me to sail.

He snorts.

Do you think Maggie would allow you to spend even one night alone with me at Tiraneering? You saw the way she watches us.

What if we got married? Eloped? We could do it now. Tomorrow we'd be married. They'd just have to put up with it.

Beware of every sentence with tomorrow in it, he says.

I don't like the way the conversation is going. I don't want to talk about the future the way he sees it. I hold onto his arm so hard I feel I'm breaking into his body. But I am happy with our snatched afternoon.

In the clay under my hand there is a perfect tiny gastropod, a miniature spiral of silica that once contained a living animal. I use a small screwdriver to scrape it out. It looks artificial. I hold it up for him. A gift. It's not a poem but it's just as beautiful.

Richard, I say, that first day why did you come out here with me? You never offered to come before.

I thought there might be a poem in it. You know, fossils, clay, time, all that stuff.

He winks at me.

Look at this little thing, he says, so perfect and it's a million years old.

More likely fifty million.

He looks at it again. Fifty million, he says. In the timescale of this little shell we don't even appear as a grain of sand.

I blush.

That's what I was thinking when we were doing it that time.

Jeannie, he says, when you go to London don't wait for me.

Do you want to split?

I want you to have a life. I don't want you to be the mistress of an old poet. Have boyfriends. Get involved. Do things. I won't be jealous. If you still want me from time to time, I'll be around.

But to a girl of seventeen that sounds like the brush-off. Along the beach there are people with sacks and hammers and trowels. In the grey light it looks like a scene from some apocalyptic film. The air is a smoky grey colour. If the ground had emitted smoke it would not have surprised me.

The poem would eventually be published as 'London Clay' in the book of that title, a Poetry Book Society Choice and winner of various prizes.

A bright twist of silica in the marl,
After fifty million years a spiral
No bigger than your nail comes to console
Us lovers drowning in impossible
Desire…

By then Grace was married, mother was dead, Maggie was gone.

The night after I gave him the fossil I dreamed that a man, a magician perhaps, entered a kind of cupboard that was elaborately bound in brass hoops, the door closed by three bolts, each padlocked, the box lifted by a crane and swung out over water on a blue nylon rope. Once the man was inside he had begun knocking to come out again. A group of bystanders laughed. I knew in my dream that this was the point of the performance, that I should find it funny, but instead I was frightened. I thought that the man really couldn't get out. I woke at that point. It was early morning. As it happened, although I did not know it until later, the knocking was the sound of Richard dragging his cases downstairs. He had taken the first boat of the day to the mainland.

Maggie told me. Maggie thought I had a soft spot for Richard. He's too old for you my dear, she said. There are plenty of boys your own age, don't waste your life on an older man.

Eleven

In our flat in Kingsland we had four rooms and they were two bedrooms, a kitchen living room, a bathroom. It was the third floor of a Victorian building. At night we heard the trains of the Northern Line. We went out, sometimes, for curry, mother liked the hottest vindaloo, and sometimes brought it home. Sometimes she went out to meetings. When I asked what they were about she said they were political but I suspected it was really group therapy. It was in the air then – anti-psychiatry and all that. David Cooper's *Death of the Family* was just out and I was devouring it.

Sometimes I met her after work and we went for a drink. You can do that here, she used to say, but at home we'd have to go in the snug. Sometimes there were sing-songs in the pub on the ground floor. *Oh Danny Boy, the pipes the pipes are calling, Daisy, daisy, give me your answer do, There'll be bluebirds over the white cliffs of Dover, Love, love me do.* We came to know the voices two floors down. I would look up from my books and catch mother's eye and groan and she would make her tight-lipped gasping face that meant, Not again. And the same cracked-voice old Irishman would sing, *Come Back to Erin mavourneen, mavourneen, come back aroon to the land of thy birth*. We could imagine him standing at the bar with his hands turned up, his eyes closed, his Guinness settling on the counter beside his Trilby. We knew he would never come back to Erin. And mother would say, Put the kettle on, there's a dear. I don't know if those old songs meant anything to her. If they brought the island back. If she ever wanted to go home again. If, when he sang *Come in the springtime, mavourneen*, she thought about the spring winds scattering the apple flowers, the first boat-load of sheep coming in to the pier and their mad scattering, the barking of seals on the Sharrav rocks, the evenings lengthening into long twilights, the light in the northern sky, the holly, the hazel, the elder and the late scrub ash with its black matchstick-tips. I did. In my mind it was the antithesis of London which stood for people and concrete and smoky nights and long days in the British Library and chips. I imagine the man downstairs thought the same way. I thought the difference between us was that I had the power to go back and he did not. I was wrong.

But what I want to say about it is this: Mother and I were happy there; she had her work, her obsessions, her bad dreams, I had my studies. We agreed on many things, food, people, politics. She never reproached me. Nobody, certainly not my father, not my sister, can say otherwise. There were times when her old self came back, chance phrases: How are you this morning mother? I'm not myself at all. And then that smile that said I know where I am and how I am. She used to say, Typical me to get it in the head; anyone else would get something normal, piles or kidney stones, but I would get insanity wouldn't I? She could make me laugh. Sometimes she called it insanity of the brain, as if there were several varieties of which she got the most embarrassing. One day she said, You better watch out. It runs in the family like wooden legs.

I laughed. And then I wondered what she meant.

And another time she said, I could never abide a notice-box and your sister was a notice-box.

Each time she said something like this she laughed as though it was meant to be funny.

You're my love-child, she said to me once, my child of Grace. I was happy when I had you in my belly. I was farting on a velvet cushion.

I thought I was the cause of all your troubles.

You were that too, she said, laughing her wild laugh. I think she cultivated it, the crazy look and the hissing laughter, she enjoyed the licence. You were all of it.

And then my sister Jeannie came to London to read Geology at King's College. It was the long Winter of Discontent. The tube didn't work. There were strikes. It rained incessantly. Callaghan was patching coalitions with anyone who would vote for him and Margaret Thatcher was sharpening her teeth. The bin men were on strike, the gravediggers were on strike, the train drivers were on strike. Where did the dead go? One expected to see them protruding stiffly from un-emptied bins or travelling infinitely in the same seat on the tube when it worked, just going round and round the underground. Or perhaps they themselves were on strike. My mother was on strike from time to time. She picketed the hospital. She gave out leaflets. She wrote articles for the *Morning Star*. We students did our bit. We marched when there were marches. We cheered the picketers. It looked like the world was falling apart and when it was reassembled there would be a place for each of us. Such hope comes only once in a lifetime, usually in youth.

I was seeing Bill Langley at the time. He had moved to the BBC, partly, he always said, to be near me. When he discovered the joys of the sea he kept a tiny plywood boat on the Crouch and we used to go down for weekends but he got tired of it after a year or two. We got married in Islington Registry just after they awarded me my doctorate. I don't know which my mother was happier about. She said I was the first person in the family actually qualified to talk about something. She was working at the Hackney Hospital then, a clerk in the pharmacy, which is how they said she came by the morphine sulphate. If that was the case, she covered her tracks exceptionally well; there was no discrepancy in her accounting. In those days it took two signatures to draw a controlled substance, and in every case the signatures were authentic.

At the time of the wedding our lives inverted. Jeannie moved in with mother and I moved out with Bill. These exchanges seemed to form the pattern of our lives. I remember that my mother welcomed the bargain with some sort of fatalism. I knew it would happen, she said. She could be guarded when she wanted to be. I think she felt abandoned. There was nothing I could do about that.

Oh well, she said to me once, I have it coming to me.

Another phrase from her collection. I have it coming to me. The devil fire you. I'm not in it at all today. They come to me still, always with a hook in my throat. I let her down in the end.

She said to me, Be true to yourself girl, whatever happens. And then, in that way she had of drifting into a different world, she said, We'll lose this fight but we won't lose forever.

I remember going to the shops with Jeannie. We were looking for clothes to get married in. Father had given me a hundred and fifty pounds and it was clear to us that anything resembling a formal dress would cost twice as much. We settled for a white broderie-anglaise gown for me, and an imitation Susie Hayward outfit for Jeannie. We blew what was left on two glasses of wine in Gordon's Wine Bar in Villiers Street.

Jeannie turned all heads, though it must be said the men were mostly gay with a professional interest in female beauty. We held our red wine in both palms, as we had heard the French did. We knew it should be warm. We felt like sophisticated sisters on a shopping spree. In the gloomy cellar that was Gordon's, smelling of must, male hormones and something from the toilets on our left, a thought slipped through my defences: Jeannie, do you think Em was Richard's?

Jeannie laughed. It was an uncomfortable laugh. Even I could see it.

I think he'd have told me, she said. She was blushing.

Oh? Is there something I should know?

She laughed again – more nervously I thought. If Em was Richard's we'd know wouldn't we?

I think we'd be the last people to know. Jeannie, do you remember the glasshouse?

I was thinking of father's memoir. At that moment I could see it on the table upstairs in the summer heat, those neatly stacked, ice-clean sheets.

What glasshouse?

The broken glasshouse. Do you remember the bits leaning against the wall of the house? Mother was planning to assemble it.

I was trying to remember what he said about it. I could hear the urgency in my own voice, though I didn't know why it was there.

She bought all the cement and the screws, I said, but the blocks for the foundation never arrived. She brought them in on Driscoll's post boat. So the glasshouse never got built. It was just the glass and the frames.

I don't know what you're talking about. I don't remember any glasshouse.

Nor me, I said. I was pleased with myself. I was right. Jeannie stared at me.

Father came to give me away. He came, as mother said he would, with a heart and a half. It seemed to me that he was never so at ease as giving me to someone else. At least Bill was pleased – although the television series had not worked out, he was still talking about doing something. Bill, I would discover, liked to keep projects in hand. He charmed everyone except father. Even my mother fell for him, though she must have recognised a reactionary and an opportunist; even I could see that. Father was charming to all of us and solicitous too. Maggie came. She looked cool and delicious. Her clipped consonants and broad vowels falling among our bastard brogues. She and mother had a long conversation. Bill's uncle was there, a cheery old soldier whose back was ruined when a landmine blew up under his jeep somewhere near Salerno. He was our best man. Nobody cried but mother took both my hands in hers outside the registry and looked at me as if she had something to say. What did I expect? Forgiveness? A blessing? Whatever was to come remained unsaid. She kissed me twice and told me I was beautiful. Afterwards we had a meal in the restaurant in the Post Office Tower. My father paid. At that time his latest was on the bestseller list, I saw copies of it on a stand at the airport. We had champagne. We toasted each other heartily, revolving above London as slowly as the world. None of us felt it but we saw that everything outside the windows was moving on.

In those days one did not say where the honeymoon was to be, but I told Jeannie and gave her an Italian number she could contact me at. In case of emergency. I told her I'd call her from time to time. Bill thought it was hilarious. Jeannie had a crush on him, he said, she used to follow him around. He thought every girl wanted him. It was part of his power.

In Naples we had a room that opened into an orange garden. It was February and a cold wind was blowing from the Apennines and beyond that from the mountains of Greece. They called it the *Grecale*.

It was a surprise to us.

We had imagined a warmer place. Nevertheless I fell in love with it. Perhaps I am drawn to coldness. In time I would learn Italian, translate from Italian, even think about buying a small house in the country somewhere. I never did, of course. I knew too much about small houses.

It was so cold that on our first day we went into town and bought warm underwear and socks. In the haberdashery, the man knew exactly what we wanted. He brought a stepladder and reached down boxes from the highest row, the just-in-case shelves. Everything came in tissue paper.

The oranges were as cold as stones but they were the brightest thing – winter's lights. It was their season. We walked a lot. I loved it, Bill did not. He was impatient with everything, he thought the people unreliable, the food too oily and sloppy, but when we closed the door on the orange garden and turned out the lights he was as happy as a child. I might have been worried by his cunning sensuality, the perfection of his pleasure. I was not much good at sex, but he didn't care. He created my body. He imagined my arousal and my satisfaction and they happened as he imagined. It may have been his experience in television that gave him this power. I was grateful for it anyway. It gave me time to learn both pretence and pleasure. I was happily full of him, rosy-cheeked at dinner, pale at breakfast. The man behind the desk approved – we called him Antonio. Bill named him one night. Naked and flabby in the cold light from the one overhead bulb, he danced and sang:

Her old hurdy-gurdy
All day she'd parade
And this she would sing,
To the tunes that it played.

Oh! Oh! Antonio, he's gone away
left me alone-ee-o, all on my own-ee-o
I want to meet him with his new sweetheart
Then up will go Antonio and his ice-cream cart

Bill's repertoire of ridiculous songs is vast. I'll say one thing for old Bill, he can make me laugh. He did the

141

hurdy gurdy handle with his prick and the ice-cream cart going up was executed with panache, turning his back to me and flipping his backside in the air like a can-can dancer.

Antonio wore beautiful shirts, whiter than white in the words of the advertisements. They seemed to glow against his skin. He was always perfectly groomed, he even shaved again in the afternoon. The girl who served us our coffee looked at us with longing. We thought she was the reason he shaved so often. She had no ring.

I collected stones for Jeannie. I picked up a piece of pumice stone on the beach. It was as light as foam. And a piece of basalt, black as the coals of Jeannie's eyes. I kept it for her. It was a time when many people did not own cameras. Our only honeymoon photograph was taken by Antonio on his Brownie box-camera. He stood back under the orange trees, stooped over the reflex lens, the strap around his neck. Two eyes, one big, one small, watched us from the box. When he pressed on the arm the shutter opened and we saw the big eye wink briefly. There we are in the unnatural and slightly garish Kodacolor, fading now, clearly happy and in love. I don't think the image is a lie. We are seated at the table where we always took our breakfast. It was just outside the dining room of the hotel, sheltered by two walls from the *Grecale* that blew in the trees overhead. The morning sun reached in there after a certain hour, its blessed warmth on our faces. I'm wearing a sweater and green flares.

My legs are crossed under the table in leather sandals. Bill is in shirtsleeves. There is coffee and bread and a bowl of fruit on the table. A white linen tablecloth. The whiteness of the walls and the fabric impress themselves rather too much. Our faces are milky by comparison. I'm laughing, Bill is making a face.

Antonio posted the print to us. No one would do it now. His real name was Enzo, it turned out. Enzo Muratore. I still have the postcard he enclosed it in. It was a photograph of Vesuvius.

One night, while we were away and she was in my sister's care, something happened and my mother crashed through her Valium and had to be sectioned. Two doctors came and certified that she was unfit to remain at home.

Jeannie had everything under control by the time we came back. She never phoned us.

It was a second breakdown. She had terrible delusions, she was paranoid, she refused all food and water, she heard voices and noises. She made accusations: we each of us were criminal in our own way, according to her, my father was a thief, I was a poisoner, Maggie was a witch, Bill Langley was an adulterer – she was right about that at least. She heard people whispering. She heard other people's thoughts and conversations between people who weren't speaking. Most of her hallucinations were auditory. Speech tormented her because she couldn't talk about the past. When I went to see her in Hackney Hospital she laughed in my face. She escaped me, she said, I couldn't touch her now. Why didn't you run while you had the chance, she said. You were the only one with a chance. Then she said, This is the poorhouse you know, I shouldn't be here at all. She was right about that too, the building used to be the Hackney workhouse.

I went to see Jeannie. She showed me my mother's room where everything that was made of glass was broken: perfume and pill bottles, wine glasses and looking glasses, picture-glass and a little glass seal she had brought from Ireland. Only the window escaped. I knew it was because breaking the window would have let the outside in, because she would lose herself in the world, she would dissolve in the vastness of elsewheres.

Why didn't Jeannie clean it up?

She said she closed the door the night mother was admitted and didn't have the heart to face it again. I saw that she was trembling. I put my arms around her even though it meant, in essence, that she was hugging me. I was the small one. When she put her arms around me I felt like a child, but she was shaking and only slowly did she calm down. I sent her out to get food and, like every big sister in the world, I set things in order again. I was comforted by the thought that this tidy room would somehow speak to mother of me, of love, of care, and that she would return to it. I imagined her listening again to the broken Irish tenor downstairs and remembering our calm evenings, our happiness, if I could dare to call it that.

Afterwards I thought that Jeannie wanted me to see it. The room and its noises and the catastrophe.

Jeannie made tea and we sat in the desolate flat listening to the sound of a football match in the bar below. If you go at weekends, she said, I'll go during the week.

They won't keep her much longer.

I can't manage her. Not on my own. Look what happened.

We only have one bedroom, Jeannie. I don't think Bill could cope with mother.

What if it happens again?

It struck me that traffic on the Kingsland Road sounded, just for that moment, like a rough sea.

What can't be cured must be endured, I said.

We stared at each other in silence for a while. Someone scored downstairs.

I said, Do you ever hear the man who sings 'Come Back to Erin'? In the pub?

Mr Kelly? He's dead. He used to be in the Post Office. He died in the Homerton. He came from Waterford. Mother visited him before … before it happened. While you were away.

There's a smell of cat's piss in here.

Jeannie sniffed the air. She got up and closed a window. There's no cat, she said. She moved around the room adjusting things, then she sat down in front of me again.

We're drifting through this, Jeannie, aren't we? We have no control over anything.

What are you on about, she snapped, you don't have to live here in this … in this pit.

I looked coolly at her. Do you mean tip, I said.

It would be months before mother came home from the poor house of Hackney. And by then I had my own troubles.

My mother died in Jeannie's arms. So Jeannie told me. We are the protagonists of our own stories. We play the hero's part, or at least the narrator's. I never believed it.

She heard, she said, a glassy barking that turned out to be my mother trying to breathe. It came from the bedroom. At first she didn't want to go in. She said my mother was a private person and needed a little cry from time to time.

Morphine sulphate represses, in the first instance, the respiratory response, the coroner's court heard. She was drowning. Jeannie called the ambulance but by the time it arrived she was already dead. There was some confusion about the time of the call. Typical NHS, Jeannie said. I could hear Maggie in the words.

Morphine sulphate is a long-acting analgesic which should not be broken, chewed, dissolved or crushed, according to the medical expert at the inquest. The consequences of any of those things, even with a normal dose, are potentially fatal. My mother had the equivalent of a week's prescription. Analysis of her stomach showed that she had taken them with, and probably mixed in, an antacid preparation called Gaviscon. It was peculiar, the coroner said, even unique in his experience. Perhaps she didn't want to upset her tummy. The Gaviscon probably disguised the taste which, if the tablets had been crushed into a paste, would have been foul. When Jeannie gave evidence he pressed her about the Gaviscon. She knew nothing about it, she said.

I told them that my mother was a socialist, that she cared for people more than things, but that people were always complicated, that she was never so happy as working at the hospital where every day she saw someone's life changed for the better. I would never have become a therapist but for her. Unfortunately, my mother had been very unhappy for a long time. I told them about my sister Em. I told them, without naming names, that Mother felt she had betrayed a lot of people. And I told them about the lonesome Irishman who sang 'Come Back to Erin' and how my mother knew she could never go back. About how she dreamed sometimes of the sea and the stones. The coroner listened patiently. I think he thought we were all mad.

Richard Wood gave evidence. He wept. The newspapers described him as the well-known Irish poet – Faber had just launched his fourth book – Irish poet's love for bestseller's suicide wife, or words to that effect. Another headline was Double Tragedy Environmentalist's Family. The rather formal word 'unrequited' occurred six times in his evidence. There was something too about the courtly love tradition. My father explained the financial arrangements he had made. The coroner, in a nice turn of phrase that my father would wish to have thought of, described them as a complicated mess of kindnesses. He meant my education, the flat, various gifts and the fact that the island house belonged to her.

Anomie is the condition of our time. We are poisoned by images, an endless sinister fallout of metaphors, full of purpose but devoid of meaning. Like any addict our means of escape is our prison; the remedy is, in fact, a deadly numbing toxin. When the time comes to feel we have lost the neural pathway. Things touch us without our knowing.

She never told me she was leaving the island to us.

And by her will Jeannie and I were to share in it.

Jeannie called me when the solicitor's letters arrived to inform us that we had become the proud possessors of less than half a deserted island. There was one key in each letter. Apparently mother had wanted us to have them, she had specified it in her will. You'll never go back, Jeannie said. I think she wanted me to sign my part away. You have your career.

But I kept my key.

Part Three

Twelve

And so there was a third and last island and it was the island of his old age. It was the island of Procida in the Bay of Naples. No more cold seas and black nights and burning stars. I went there for his seventieth birthday and to meet his third wife. Bill had finally got around to making something with my father in it. Don't mess it up for me Grace, he said, don't fuck it up. He was bringing a documentary crew. They would arrive a few days after me. Richard Wood would be there. My father's new wife would be visiting her parents for the first days of my stay. They lived in Genoa, far to the north, several train journeys away. It was, he told me in his letter, as if in exculpation, the city that made him fall in love with her, the centre dominated by the *caröggi*, the dark narrow streets that wind around the old port. He went there to talk to the architect Renzo Piano about the living roof structures he was building and she was there in the office. It was love at first sight for both of them, he said.

Piano piano, as they say. But not for you Father.

I have begun to talk to myself. How long has this been going on? Don't answer that.

I passed through the suburbs of Naples where the pavements were blocked with refuse. The taxi driver apologised. He had seen people shooting rats in his *rione*, he said. Berlusconi is a *cazzo*, he's taking us back to the Dark Age, he said, the fascists are back. He clenched his fist and shook it at the grey glass of the windscreen.

The little island ferry came through the entrance and immediately began to slow down. She made a slight turn about three hundred metres out and dropped an anchor. Then she pulled against the anchor chain and that resistance turned her so that the stern was towards the land. It was a graceful and gallant manoeuvre, a curtsy. There are three islands, he told me on the phone, take care that you don't fall asleep in the ferry or you'll end up visiting all three in turn. It was the afternoon and the ferry was quiet. I could really have slept to the beat of the engine and the sea.

He met me at the Port Captain's Office. I scarcely recognised him. He had a grey beard and his hair was white as Formica.

He drove me up through the narrow lanes of the island, crazy with Fiat Puntos and motor scooters and pedestrians who shrank away from the traffic, and we came to a place where he could park his car. We went in a gate and there was the garden and the house. It was not what I expected.

He brought me upstairs and showed me a room. Come down when you're ready, he said, and we'll have a drop of wine.

There were two windows. In the distance was the sea, the haze of the mainland, the old broken back of Vesuvius. That old mountain had done enough damage in its time.

The house was plainer, older than I thought it would be. It was emptier too. Quieter. The road below my window was narrow and across the way there was a lemon grove, a single old kitchen chair in the shade. An old woman walked through it carrying a watering can and a hoe. She wore a straw hat. Among the distant gardens, the cicadas were bitter about the heat. The geckos waited for evening. They looked on human existence as a temporary interruption in the hegemony of stone. They stopped for hours in one place and then on some geodetic sign shifted like a clockwork toy. There was no difference between the new station and the old, no difference in light or air, no obvious reason for change. At night they cavorted after insects and made weird upside-down leaps onto cornices or street lamps.

The table stood under a square frame over which the vines crossed. In clusters the pale grapes caught shafts of sunlight. The shade was delicious. A wooden ladder stood against the frame at one side. The table was of wood too, rough-hewn enough, a country table, but the chairs were plastic. He brought a tray containing two glasses of wine, some olives, some bread. I said that the gardens are magical.

Yes. They all have one. The island of gardens.

He made a gesture that was intended to encompass everything.

There's an old lady across the street from my bedroom watering her vegetables.

They do that. There's never enough rain.

I was glad to have seen her. The earth is important still.

He nodded. He agreed with that.

So tell me about you, he said. How are you? How are you faring?

Without ever having thought of the idea before I said, I'm shipwrecked.

He laughed. Then he frowned. Bill?

Bill, yes.

So how are you managing it?

I took a deep breath. I said I was coping but things were coming to a head.

And if you don't mind, I don't like talking about it.

As you wish.

Something lapidary in the light, every shadow edged, exact, more itself than before. He put his hand on the nape of my neck. It fitted there. I had the feeling that he too was on the verge of revelation but that he turned away at the very last.

Instead he said, Come and look at Salvatore's rabbits.

He was up again, leaving the wine and food. He looked unsettled. There was something nervous and disturbing about him. He led me out under the grapes. There were walls, shallow steps that led nowhere, wisteria, bougainvillaea trailing everywhere, the thick tonguey leaves of the magnolia, the grapes, the lemon trees, the chipped statue of an armless Venus surrounded by cactus – an installation, he told me, one of Serena's, the statue and the cactus had to be read together, the whole situation a totality. He didn't sound convinced.

Only the blue sky suggested that there was a world beyond. So this was his new island, his walled paradise. Once there was sea now there was stone. He was always longing to be outside.

We went down to where the vines spiralled onto old branches slung between posts and tied with rags. Salvatore – their neighbour who looked after the house when they travelled – kept them and had the grapes. He made wine with them. It had to be drunk young, a small wine like all the locals, but quite good. Then in a slatted shade there was a stone oven big enough almost to get my shoulders into. Again Salvatore built it. The Centane stone was famously hard. Then an orchard of stunted lemon and orange trees. The fruits were last year's crop and not good for eating, they had been on the tree over winter and the cold spring winds dried them out, and the new fruit was small and hard and green still. I remembered those winds.

Through a gap in the wall he brought me to where his neighbour kept rabbits and hens in cages.

He looked at me ruefully. They really are almost self-sufficient, the islanders. They have to be.

Food that travels further than the length of a parish isn't worth eating?

He started. I could see he was trying to remember. So many books, how could he remember one line.

He said: It's a funny thing, people quoting your own work back at you.

I know.

I don't like it.

There were pumpkins growing in the floor of a half-finished house and basil plants and rosemary, a fig tree with tiny hard fruits and a twisted olive tree whose trunk had split in two maybe a hundred years before; the ghost of the second half seemed necessary to sustain its precarious balance.

It was the kind of garden that could be found in any house on the island that had the space, he said, as all the older ones did. Everybody grew their own food, if they could. But it was all changing now. They have a saying, *Stavamo meglio quando stavamo peggio*. We were better when we were worse.

He collected half a dozen eggs and I made a basin of my shirt and he put them into it. And standing there, with a shirtful of eggs, and looking at him I said, Once upon a time I wanted to kill you.

He stared at me. He didn't say anything. He still held an egg in each hand. There were four in my shirt. If, for

156

example, he had embraced me suddenly we would have broken everything.

We went out for dinner early. I could see he didn't want to be alone in the house with me. He may have been hoping I wouldn't come. The streets were heavy with petrol fumes and dust. It was not yet evening but already I saw mosquitoes drifting against the shade, subtle specks of unease. They suck your blood and feed the kids, hardly a neighbourly thing to do. I went into a chemist shop and bought a spray. He didn't seem to be bothered by them, but perhaps he had armed himself before we left. We went to a place called Bar Giorgio and sat outside. It was, he said, the best pizza on the island. We could see the wood fire; no one sat inside because of its heat. We talked about the economy (the Camorra is behind every big project – he pointed to a new marina under construction), about Berlusconi in his second incarnation (he is the future of every European state) and the difficulty the island had in coming to terms with recycling and not burning their waste. You could see the bonfires early in the morning, he said, and in certain conditions the air was unbreathable. It was a depressing evening. I wondered why he would choose to live in a place he cared so little about. I thought that perhaps his cynicism was a way of distancing himself from me. Disdain is a glittering shield. It hurts even to see it.

I never bother to remember dreams. Despite my training, or perhaps because of it, I don't really believe in them.

They have always seemed to me to be essentially trivial, housekeeping for the brain or at best an exercise in poetics. But that first night on the island I dreamed that I was looking in the windows of a car and it was like looking into a fish tank. My father was there, floating like an astronaut or a baby in a womb. The light was green and uncertain. His head was too big and his eyes were pearlescent and unresponsive. He might have been blind like a puppy. He was wearing the ochre-coloured canvas trousers that he used to wear when we were children; it was wet and the thinness of his legs showed through. Why had his legs become so thin? His arms too. I felt a surge of terrible pity. It came to me that the glass would not break because of the pressure – I had seen something to that effect in a film or television programme, people trying to break out of a car underwater – so I simply looked on as he floated. He moved with wonderful grace, in slow motion, without any sign of pain or fear. I knew, as I watched, that I should be happy for him. If I broke the glass he would wash out into our world and things would begin again. But, in fact, when the first pity vanished it was replaced by revulsion and anger. I was the one who felt pain, who felt suffocated. I was drowning for him. I had to break the glass or die. I began to look for a weapon.

I got up and stood at my window.

There were two coffee cups a little jug of boiled milk and an espresso pot, a copy of yesterday's *Telegraph* (it's all they get here) folded to the crossword. The curdled skin on the milk like a drift of burnt plastic. There was a little bowl of white butter, already losing its shape in the heat, a plate of bread, two pieces of pastry. They were called *lingua di bue*, he said, which means ox tongue. They were a speciality of the place. They looked lascivious enough. We sat down to breakfast. I had seen photographs of him sitting here. I remember one page-length feature; the theme was, Radical critic finds peace at last.

He looked deflated, like a balloon that had cooled, and I thought there was a pallor in his tan, something chemical almost, and a dry slack skin.

Are you all right?

Yes, I'm all right, I'm fine, I'm not sleeping well that's all.

Is there something wrong?

Old age has laid her hand on me. Do you know the song? Frank Harte. Richard and I used to know him. I expect he's dead now.

Go on, Grace, ask him now, I thought. There's no time like the present. I took a deep breath, but he spoke first.

What you said yesterday, about wanting to kill me …

Tell me about your life here, I said. He looked relieved.

So he told me things about the island instead of himself. That it was formed in the eruptions of the Phlegrean Fields, twelve thousand years ago, and is really no more than the joined rims of three volcano

159

craters. Jeannie knows all about that, he said, if we could risk getting her going. He said it was the most densely populated rural area in the world; that the walled village at the southern end used to contain a penitentiary, now a community centre, and that consequently it was a closed island until 1967 and you needed a *permesso* just to land, and that it was one of the places that Mussolini exiled communists to; that the architecture of the houses was remarkable and unique, more Africa than Europe; that the dialect was impenetrable.

It was a hollow kind of knowledge, I saw, a tourist's *précis*. It told me nothing.

A language is a world, I said, the unconscious is a language without a grammar. You'll never belong here, you'll never understand these people though you may think you can. You can never experience things the way they do. You can never dream their dreams. You can't even feel the same sun on your face. You'll always be a stranger.

I know, he said, I always have been. And you?

There was a ticking sound in the garden but everything was still. I knew that whatever happened now had already happened before, that every moment had its double, that in fact every moment was dual, containing both directions, both positive and negative, yes and no, that everything had both happened and not happened. It was true I had never felt at home, but I didn't want him to know, him of all people. I wanted him to feel homeless. I wanted him to believe that we all had anchors and he was the restless one, drifting through our moorings, alone. Unbidden a line from his book came to me. How did it return after all these years of repression? He wrote: Jane was faithful to nothing and no one except place; not men, not hope, not dreams, but to an island.

Once there was an island, I said. You weren't there.

I meant we had a home once. We had lost it, but it was there in memory. It was our home not his.

But he shrugged. All my life you've been shrugging me off, father. But not anymore. There's no stepping off this island where you find yourself in the end. You've had your day.

You imagined that, he said, you were an exile, we all were, except maybe Jane.

On a wire that ran from a pole to the roof of the house I saw a sparrow with its wings slightly open. All my childhood he was the one who put us in words. He had the copyright of our most private thoughts. Because he owned our utterance we performed it. In the book that never was he said my mother was a careless woman who brought her children up like animals. He wrote that she was a big-boned handsome woman, generous in everything, gentle in nothing; copious, unpredictable, like a happening in nature, a storm or a flood or a downpour. It might have been a form of praise unknown to me. She took men when she needed them, he said, and he was one. He never said that she had a brain.

He wrote that a parent never forgives herself for the death of a child. There was a long passage about

161

blamelessness that was really about blame. He forgave her but she was lost forever in the interstices of guilt and desire. His forgiveness could not pass to her. And there was no return.

Yet I saw that he yearned most of all to be Richard Wood, gliding in on a breeze, anchoring in the lucid water, taking the woman, making the poems. He wanted more than anything to be an itinerant maker, like an old man we used to see beating old copper cylinders into pots and polishing them, who came and went in the country on some calendar of his own imagining. My father was continually handling beautiful things, exquisite phrases and ideas, but they were borrowed. He poisoned them and they passed from hand to hand, elegant but dangerous devices. Slogans not poems. When my father wanted to talk about remorse it was unbearable, in the book that never was, it was an obscenity, a human organ grafted to a stone, a pietà stitched with a bleeding breast. Sitting in the train in the burning waterless landscape of 1976, between Guildford and Woking, I saw that he had cut me off from her, that I could never be in her thoughts again, that he had waved his witch's wand and made her an émigré in the islands. He had reduced her voice to a babble. In the book that never was.

His children? He said we only wore clothes when we were told to. We fought like spitting cats. We killed birds and fish. In the night-time echoing island we prowled and pried and discovered everything. We inherited her casual sexuality. I was beyond help, but younger Jeannie could be saved. Our mother's madness lay before us. He might have said, Intemperance is naturally punished with diseases. He might have said, What good were eyes to me?

It was a tissue of signs. It was, as always, himself, the book that never was. In a moment, in the sunlight from the high glass roof, in beautiful Waterloo Station, I held his life to be burgled, it was mine to dispose of. All I remember is joy. The bin was full. I remember there was the bottom half of a dried-up ham sandwich. The yellow of the mustard.

I said, The simple truth is we all hate you.

He smiled. It surprised me. He wore a round-necked T-shirt. When he smiled the scalene muscles hung like ropes from his cheek to his chest. His skin was mottled and cracked. There were purple shadows under his eyes. Only his lips seemed to have become fuller and richer and more sensual with age. They were red now, like a girl's.

No, he said, you know that's not true. It's what you felt at the time, but you of all people know that the opposite is the case.

I shook my head.

We got over all that.

No, he said again. I gave you a childhood like no other. Jane and I, we created that island, a colony of peace and strength in a world that was about to annihilate itself. You never feared the bomb, like other children. When people elsewhere in the world were building bomb shelters you were swimming in the ocean. You never learned the commodity fetish from television. You were free spirits. You are what you are because of that. It was a gift that few children of your generation were given.

Hippies, I said. What did you give us? Look at us, we're the unhappiest family in the world.

He smiled again. You say that, but you know it's not true. You, of all people, you know exactly what the balance of happiness and unhappiness is.

It's true if I say it's true.

He shook his head. He moved the cup on the table. He looked down and up again.

None of us is a whole person, I said, our hearts are broken.

Child, he said, you have no idea.

I saw that his hand was shaking. He moved the cup again and I saw the slightest tremor. We notice these things, a professional skill, we swimmers in other people's psyches. He was controlling it as best he could. I might have pitied him. At his age pity is the same as love. Or it's enough. It is the end encoded in the beginning. The end of the law of the father.

Why did you never have children with Maggie?

He looked away.

I already had two.

Three, I said.

He was silent for a time. Then he looked at me. His eyes were pinched and dry. What was he afraid of? Now, I thought, there will be more lies. But he just turned away.

I walked the island lanes, thinking it through, thinking about him. It meant I didn't have to watch him sulk. I climbed through streets that turned into private roads that forced me to retrace my steps and start again; that wound in and out and then stopped unpredictably; that ended in gates, in doorways, in views over the sea or over the edge. The houses crowded down on each other, built across the path, overhanging me. There were external staircases that climbed sharply or doubled back on each other like tricks of perspective; low roofs that I could look down on from the road, rounded half-barrels; doors that seemed let into cliffs, doors set at an angle to the street or the path; square, round or trapezoid windows; elaborate shutters, door knockers, gates. Nothing was straight. Nothing was simple. It was a demented geometry. It was as though the inhabitants had built outwards from some conception of the interior, of the heart or the soul, of the placing of furniture, of opportunities provided by shade or by an irregularity in time or space, as though the world did not exist except as a shell for the inside. I thought if I could do that with my life. Begin at some space that was my own and build out into the light. But I am walled and roofed by other people's words and the walls grow inwards to fill the space. I am drowning inside.

If I could only touch someone.

There were stagnant pools, a smell of stagnant water and detergent. A smell of other people's food. If I went in I would emerge in someone else's life. I only needed the courage. But when I looked down the narrow corridors I saw old women and men impassive as troglodytes. They belonged to an underworld that stubbornly remained attached by life or love and through which doors and light and gifts passed forward and back.

I walked into evening. Old men in doorways watched me pass. Women on chairs outside their shops. They saw a strange pale woman walking too fast. And that was me. I saw myself in their eyes. Who would want me? My hips had never held a child. What future could I have? What value is there in a solitary life?

In the lengthening shadows everyone was out of doors. People greeted each other as though they had not met in years. It was a parable of concord. So many people lived here on this little heap of black and pumice stone that if they did not meet for a day they considered each other lost. When they embraced it was an affirmation that existence could be continued invisibly, that one could not imagine everything that might befall a neighbour. Every one of them was part of a web of tensile cousinships, adulteries, parishes, friendships, districts. The relationships stretched backwards to the names on gravestones, forward into putative births and laterally into the remote distance. I thought: This is how the island makes itself the world; complexity is its signature; without it no one could live here; it would become like the empty islands of home, places where life had become too simple. This was the mirror of our island. There was never an undisclosed action, never an empty gesture, no secret.

The island was heavy with sound, every happening had its equivalent in the air. I remember bells, birdsong ending exactly at sunset, talk, calling, conversations carried out over long distances, window to window or across streets, indiscrete conversations in gardens and backyards and kitchens, the sound of cutlery or delft, chatter on the overloaded buses, mobile phones ringing, dogs watching my approach, barking.

I was thinking that Bill would arrive with his camera crew and his questions and his false bonhomie. I thought of an insect trapped in a net, a butterfly or a mosquito – the spider's web is five times stronger than steel, weight for weight, the insect no more than an unlikely combination of down and wire.

Somewhere my father was brooding, waiting. In his island paradise at long last.

Death too. That gentleman was patient. He waited for the next comer in his best suit.

But not for me this time. Fathers do not live forever. We wait our turn, but they go first.

Thirteen

When I get his call I drive up to see Maggie. Ask her to come, Jeannie, you know I can't do it. It is one of those summer evenings when Oxford glows like old gold. The colleges turn their backs on the town and face resolutely towards lighthearted young students in boats with champagne bottles trailing over the side. Here, they say in their incurable Anglo-Saxon muddle-headedness, is the future, whether we like it or not. And young women cycle the streets on Roadsters as though they were re-enacting a film about themselves. There is something incorrigibly of a *construct* about Oxford, a great edifice built to look like itself, a parody that excludes all parody, something intended by history to look important and intellectual, a spectacle. We in the London colleges, of course, believe that the baton has long since passed to us and that all the exciting work is happening on our streets and classrooms. Time will tell, as it always does – whether it's telling the truth or not.

I get there early as always and drive straight into town and spot a lucky parking space outside Blackwell's.

I attach myself to a tour going into Trinity and sit in the Lawns to wait. It is a beautiful evening. There is no place in the world like Oxford on a fine evening.

Another tour comes out of the quad and I see that the young man leading it is a former student of mine. He recognises me and comes over at once. I remember you, I say. You got a first. What are you doing giving guided tours of ancient institutions?

He looks embarrassed. I'm trying to get it together for a PhD. I've not had much luck. They promised me tutoring.

That's something at least. What's the thesis?

I'm looking at the feedback effects between climate change and volcanic activity, he says. The North-Eastern Greenland ice-stream, that kind of thing. Crustal heat flow and the effect of the rock topography on heat distribution.

Right on the button, I say. Up to the minute. They're all worried about that. You'll get funding, never fear.

Hope so. Otherwise I'm dead.

Better hurry though, Greenland may well be green by the time you finish your thesis.

He doesn't laugh. I always remember the serious ones, the eager earnest ones; the jokers are two-a-penny. He looks away down the path toward Parks Road. I notice that his hands are pale and his nails are bitten to the quick. He clenches them briefly, sharply, then releases them slowly.

How is your sister? Dr Langley.

Do you know her?

Well, I had a … She helped me once. I had bit of a breakdown. Bad one actually. Back in second year. It didn't last long. It was just a student thing, you know, these things …

I didn't know that.

No, I didn't tell anyone. Now that it's over I feel I can talk about it.

He is clenching his hands and straightening them again. Now I notice that his fingers are exceptionally long and thin. Piano-fingers, Maggie would have called them.

I think I was eating too much tuna.

He smiles at me and I laugh. Is that bad for you?

I was eating a lot of it. I was broke, you know. I lived on John West. Tuna in brine. Mostly with pasta. It has everything, unfortunately everything includes high levels of mercury. Think earth-science student gets heavy metal poisoning and you can see the irony.

Again that direct smile.

That's a good one.

A cracker, he says. My heart was going like the clappers, I was sweating like a pig, I was going blind. Well, I wasn't seeing things right.

And Grace, my sister, diagnosed this?

Well, no. I looked it up myself. Once I stopped the tuna I started to get better. Dr Langley treated me for the symptoms. I was depressed. We got along quite well. She didn't accept the tuna theory at all, but I knew what I was talking about. They're well up the food chain, you see, and levels of methyl mercury accumulate in the tissue. Mercury poisoning is a well-known side effect of eating a lot of tuna. Of course it's easily mistaken for a whole sack of other things. It's a crap disease I'll say, but it's not insanity or bipolar or whatever. I am a qualified earth scientist after all.

A geologist.

That's it. I should know about heavy metals, shouldn't I?

Certainly.

Well, there you are.

What did Grace say about the tuna?

Displacement. She called it displacement. Crap of course.

Your tour is becoming restless.

He looks at them. They have clustered near a mediaeval-looking striped tent. There are stools and a microphone stand inside. It looks both completely incongruous and absolutely necessary. The thought occurs to me that it was Oxford itself.

Bastards, he says, fucking Japs. What a crap job. They need to take pictures of everything. Please Mr Guide can I take you picture with this velly old tlee.

Well, I say, I see the tuna turned you into a racist as well.

The Missing Bean in Turl Street. Maggie likes the atmosphere here, she likes to be with the young people.

171

We look around approvingly at the young students on their laptops or poring over books or chatting to other young people with piles of books on the table. It fits some model of what an Oxford café should look like, almost a parody of itself.

It's so Oxford don't you think, Maggie says, as if she had read my mind.

I'd have preferred the Isis, I say.

Oh no, she says, much too hippy.

While we queue I tell her about my encounter with the ex-student. I never noticed him going mad, I say, you'd think I of all people would recognise the signs, I can't believe it, he was in all my lectures. We take our coffees to a quiet corner. She looks well. Even when I was a teenager she didn't have a young look, conventionality made her middle-aged but it also preserved her in that time and she hadn't aged since then, a kind of permanent, improbable thirty-five. She thinks I look wonderful, that academic life obviously suits me, which is a surprise really, they never thought my stones would turn into this, because she always thought I would end up working for Shell, or even for someone like Sidney.

How is Sidney?

Oh, Sidney is always Sidney. Busy busy busy. He's in Ghana as we speak.

Once I'd asked her what Tom thought of her new husband. She told me they hated each other. You must understand, my dear, that Sidney makes a living in a very simple way, he imports aluminium in seventy-five kilo ingots and melts them down and makes what he laughingly calls added-value products, and the whole process is, according to your father, exactly the thing that has us where we are, namely destroying the planet. He compared it to the Triangle Trade in slaves. Frankly he went too far.

She'd had it very clear then. I don't think she ever had such a firm grasp of what Tom's work was about. In a way, what he did wasn't really work at all. Sidney, on the other hand, was a businessman or an industrialist or an importer – all clearly delineated activities with nothing of the fuzzy boffin world about them. She never mentioned words like smelter, dross, carbon emissions. Sidney worked, as far as she was concerned, in a world of alchemy where used aluminium turned into money by some magically sterile and isolated process. Saving the planet was all very well in its way, but somebody had to keep the show on the road. Her father's thinking was still the scantlings of her world – he made his money on agricultural implements, metallurgy in her blood in one way or another. Tom married me for my money, she used to say. It was a joke once. After the divorce she never said it again.

What news Jeannie? Something good I hope, I rather need it at the moment. Have you and Richard decided to tie the knot?

I got a call from Tom this morning. He's in Italy, as you know. The fact is he's married again. An installation artist that he met in some architect's office. She's twenty something.

A wave of some kind passed over her face. It might have been pain or anger. Or contempt. Or pity.

I reach across the table and catch her right hand and, so quickly I almost didn't see it happen, she covers mine with her left. In that instant the current reverses and I am transported back to the time when I was comforted rather than comforter. Don't waste your time on older men, I heard her saying.

Tears come but I can do nothing about it.

After a time I say, It's his seventieth birthday. He wants us all to come to meet her.

Stupid bastard.

I thought you might feel that way.

Oh, she says angrily, lifting her hand and sweeping something invisible from between us, He was always unfaithful.

She leaves the old-fashioned word hang in the coffee-heavy air.

Somehow I knew it, she says. Always. I don't know how I settled down into that bloody bovine house on that bloody bovine island arranging flowers and sending people thank you cards and entertaining his publisher and all that bally nonsense. That was his fantasy of a writer's life. What absolute tosh. Can you believe it, a grown man?

She has made a fist, a blue-veined, childish fist with a gold ring shaped to imitate a piece of tree bark on the top. She looks at it and slowly loosens the fingers.

He gave me this ring, she says, Sidney hates it. I can only wear it when he's away.

The café stills around us. Not that anybody has been so impolite as to notice her distress. It's just how I feel it. Nothing is happening, suddenly, like those brief moments in a storm when, inexplicably, there is no wind. Behind the counter the staff are leaning on things or looking at their mobile phones. The customers are between lifting cups and putting cups down. A man on the street is looking at a notice in the window. What is it about? It looks like a planning notice. Another is waiting for the pedestrian light.

He asked you to tell me. He couldn't tell me himself. He could have written a bloody letter. Do they have a postal system in Italy anymore? Anyway, it's irrelevant. Come to think of it, that's probably what he thinks too.

It seems she's heard all about me. She's even read some of my papers. He wants us to be friends.

Oh fuck it, Maggie says. Let's get out of here.

I've never heard her swear before.

She said: He once told me — this was during the divorce — that I was boring. I thought it was so unfair. Because being married to him was boring and living on that bloody island was boring. You know why women fall for him? Because despite all of his mad notions and changing the world and all that he's just plain comfortable. He has a comfortable face and he makes comfortable love. I can't imagine him dragging a woman into a forest or tearing his clothes off and diving into a river naked. There's nothing Tarzan about him at all. I often think his idea of nature is really a wild patch in someone's back garden. He just wants everybody to have a wild patch. And you know, the most hurtful thing was that he compared me to your mother. Oh why do we have to remember the worst things. It's so unseemly.

We wanted to walk and for some reason we turned left at the door and so we find ourselves in High Street. Maggie's face is pale. She leans into me and I take her arm. I find it strange to be the strong one.

You shouldn't hold it against him, I say. You know we're all damaged one way or another.

Well I think it's time to put it behind you. Time to straighten your back.

You weren't there.

She pulls away from me and stops dead in the street. That's what he said all the time! Of course I wasn't there. Am I somehow responsible for that? Is it my fault too? Because I was in London having a good time while your Emily was falling off a cliff on some godforsaken island? That was the sixties. Do you have any idea what London was like in the sixties? I had boys queuing at my door before he came along. I wasn't on your island. I was in a bedsit in Kensington and I wasn't bloody alone.

No, that's not what I mean …

But it's what it does mean. You're all twisted up with blame and guilt. As far as I can see Grace is the only normal one.

But Grace killed her. They were always playing on the tower.

Immediately I regret it. I turn away from her stare. I feel panic rising. The Iffley Road bus is passing. On the top deck someone catches my eye and waves. It's the mad young geologist. Suddenly I remember him after class one day, waiting until the room was empty to say that he had met my sister. Absurdly I thought they were having an affair. I remember that I laughed and walked away. I may have said something. He never approached me again.

I'm sorry I said that, Maggie, it's not really true.

She takes a deep breath, puts her hand on my arm. Again that current of comfort.

Be careful of Grace, she says. She hates everyone, especially your father. She blames him.

She's my sister.

She's brittle. I can see her breaking down. Of course shrinks are prone to nerves anyway. I remember that time she came down to visit, I was afraid for her. Poor Bill, he didn't know what he was letting himself in for.

Bill takes care of himself.

You may be right. I like old Bill. He's never short of a smile or a kind word.

He's a charmer, I say, but she misses the irony. She smiles.

Yes, she says, he's that and all.

We watch a bus driver helping an elderly woman find her walking stick.

You'll go to Italy of course, Maggie says. Tell him I hope he gets the pox from his artist.

Again she takes me by surprise.

Richard tells me that he's got his call too. I knew he was in Ireland, we had spoken a few weeks before, but we hadn't been together in almost a year.

It is the long goodbye, he says. It will be the last time I'll see him.

Don't be so melodramatic, I tell him, I'm not your audience.

He laughs.

Oh, he says, everyone is an audience, that's the curse of being a poet for too long. You become addicted to aphorising.

Well aphorise to yourself for once.

But still Jeannie, I can't shake the feeling, the dread really, that this will be the last time I see Tom.

His sight is going, we both know that. In due course he will only be able to see things sideways. When he first told me he joked that he had never seen straight anyway.

The line is bad. It's raining in Tiraneering and that translates as static. Four hundred miles of cable and all the technology and still it finishes at a wooden pole in the roadside scrub-ash and whitethorn a hundred yards from the Atlantic. I might as well have the Atlantic itself on the line for the weird spitting and gravelly sucking. Richard's melancholy brings with it a Greek chorus from a half-tide rock in a gale of wind, or one of those strange harsh and erotic Gaelic laments that he loved, beautiful and flawed as a fossil loosened from clay.

I'll see you there, he says.

That'll be something at least. I miss you.

Me too. I have a lot to tell you.

Fourteen

My father's new wife came. She was a delicate, courteous young woman. She called me *Cara Grazia*, delighted that I could speak her language, however badly. At first I thought, a little resentfully, that she was punning on my name. I had forgotten that Grace and gratitude are linked by a common root. She dressed in dark neat clothes, her hair cut close to her head. She looked like a bundle of self-composure in a tight package. I had noticed before that Italian women, growing up in a chauvinist society, learned to be either docile or assertive. She spoke English in a limited way. She fed me olives and cool wine. She had heard about my trouble. These matters were so difficult. She hoped everything would be for the best. When I said something long and important about marriage she asked to have it translated. My father, I noticed, spoke in two tenses, the present and the recent past. A lazy grammarian. I could have translated as well myself. He did not look at me. Later when he had gone to bed she asked me if I had said something to upset him, he was sad, he was very sad. And angry too. The Italian word for angry is *arrabbiato*. People think it has something to do with intemperate Arabs, but it derives in fact from the Latin for rabid or raving. We saw the light come on in their room, we saw him close the shutters. I said we had disagreed about the past. She shook her pretty head. *Il passato*, she said. She made a puffing sound with her lips and a small explosive gesture with her fingers. It meant the past was gone. Young people can strike such poses. I saw its plume blowing away through the lemon grove. She made it sound so easy. I loved her for it. But I knew the ash would settle in the shadows. It would be there to mark us when we had forgotten it.

If only I had not hated my father I could have loved this woman. But then the world would have had to be recast, my sister and mother saved, my father a true father and husband not a shadow on the kitchen floor. None of us steps into the same sea at the same time, and tomorrow we cannot ourselves step in it. Even the cells of our bodies are not the same today as yesterday. But what we hold in our hearts remains stony and intransigent. I looked at her from a great distance and wanted to be like her. And I knew I would hurt her.

Jeannie came next day.

My father didn't want to go down to the harbour – he wasn't feeling well, he said – so I met her from the ferry and drove her to the house. Where's Daddy? I don't know Jeannie, he said to collect you. He always meets me. Well not today.

So she had been here before. Of course. She got him and I got mother. And all that goes that road.

Her hair seemed blacker than before. She had my mother's eyes, black as jet. In the sunshine she had the simplicity of a statue. She was wearing an Armani dress. She picked it up at an airport, she said, Paris, or maybe Rome. Her toenails were painted lime. They looked like one of her precious stones. Would you like a coffee, Jeannie? Yes please, would you mind boiling the milk?

Then came Bill. He was in tropical kit, he said. He wore his white linen suit. The camera crew were staying at the Hotel Riviera and he thought he should stay with them but I knew it was because his researcher was there. This was not new. I almost divorced him once, for playing away, as he liked to call it, but then my mother died and after that I got used to it. Habit, as someone said, is a great deadener.

He stayed with us.

He told me in our bedroom that Jeannie had the kind of good looks that frightened men. He didn't fancy being in Richard's place. Imagine waking up in the morning with Cruella De Vil in the bed. Oh Cruella let's make poetry together. Not today dear, I'm studying this rock.

Oh shut up Bill.

He was excited, he said, about the prospect of finally doing something serious. The old man was a talker and the island would make a great setting. Radical finds peace in idyllic island, the vines, the *trattoria*, the narrow lanes, you know. He had a whole narrative of how my father's life had gone, from early political activism to a Zen-like composure in old age. The human interest was overwhelming. He was thinking about music and liked the idea of Bach cello suites, what did I think? They were deep, emotionally moving. He could talk crap like that for hours on end. But he knew his music, give him his due. He could hum the Bach. Suite 1 in G, he said. This is the *Courante* – it'll be perfect. He hummed it now, waving his right hand to indicate the time. He sang in St Luke's Chelsea church choir of all things. *Te Lucis Ante Terminum*, rendered with gusto as if he believed in a plea to the creator to protect him through the night. Bill the Blessed and his angelic voice. He was probably fucking the sopranos.

Bald and fattening now, in bed he looked like a dead seal. His skin smelled slightly smoked. I told him he would have to stop wearing slimfit shirts but he didn't listen to me. I told him he needed to get out of his car and walk. Precepts that might serve him well in the future.

Look at you, he said to me, you need to think body image.

This was how we expressed our hatred. In metaphor.

Where is the old man?

I said he was probably in his room. Something was eating him.

Don't tell me you upset him, I could do without family issues for god's sake.

He'll get over it, I said. Ask him if he thinks the Greens undermined the left because they gave capitalism a way to save face? Ask him if he thinks the Greens are the vegetarian bourgeoisie – that's what mother used to call them. Ask him …

Oh shut up Grace, it's a bloody documentary not a show trial.

Ask him if he thinks vegetables will save the world.

He chuckled at that. If he hadn't been such a hopeless shit where women were concerned we might have made a go of it. If his ego hadn't needed so much feeding.

Then came Richard Wood. He kissed me and looked at me. You haven't changed at all, he said. He put his arm around my waist as we walked to the car. I carried his laptop bag. He kept glancing at it. I was supposed to notice something.

It's a memoir, he said.

Will your old *Iliad* be in it?

I've never sold her, you know? I can't bring myself to do it. She's rotting in one of the old hay sheds. It's pity to the gods.

And the island, and our house, and the seabirds and the whales?

Everything.

And mother? And your love affair? And how she ended up in the madhouse?

He sucked air through his teeth. It was hard to decide what it meant. He did not look at me but studied the way a driver in a Fiat Punto who attempted to down-face a bus had become trapped against the wall of the narrow street and was about to lose both wing mirrors.

Then, as if I had not asked the question at all, he went on: I finally abandoned the pen for prose but I'm a two-fingered typist. I don't type so much as peck. I feel like a blackbird stabbing at worms. The blackbird is the garden's fascist. Do you think a great poem could be written on a computer, for God's sake?

He shook his head and watched the Punto go past with both mirrors intact.

Never, he said, almost to himself. It won't be about me, of course, that'd be a failure of taste. It'll be about all the people in my life. All the people who've meant something to me, my influences, all that.

He was excited he said. He was hoping to have a long chat with my father. He wanted to double-check things. He didn't want to write anything that wasn't true. Of course he knew all about the memoir-is-fiction-debate. He waved his hand dismissively, as if the matter had been settled to his satisfaction in the recent past. He quoted V. S. Pritchett to the effect that it was all in the art, that you don't get any credit for living. He talked all the way to the house. Jeannie met him at the gate. I had the impression she was waiting just inside. He kissed her too, but he didn't tell her that she hadn't changed.

Perhaps he saw too much of her. I saw my father at the window watching us.

Where is Bill?

Jeannie said he left shortly after me. She said he mentioned research.

She couldn't stop herself.

They all knew. Public knowledge. Bill and his bit of fluff. Good old Bill. Life in the old dog yet. The men certainly admired him for it. They all wanted it. Look at my father and his Italian. Richard and Jeannie. How old was Jeannie when they first started? She never told me. My mother was the love of his life until Jeannie was old enough to take her place. And what did Jeannie think? It was possible she didn't know. She knew more about stones than hearts. I looked at my father and saw that he knew. He pitied me. I did not want his pity.

And Richard Wood wanted to know all about the film. In the space of four sentences he used the terms *mise en scene*, *montage* and *level of immediacy*; of course documentary film has a level of immediacy that a book can never have etc. I had never heard Bill use any of them. I saw that he wanted badly to be in it. He had done his homework. Jeannie said Bill was sure to interview him. She suggested that he might read some of his poems. I didn't say that even if he filmed them they would never make it past the first edit. Bill didn't get poetry or friendship.

Richard said he was thirsty and very hot. Jeannie went and got him a glass of water. He sat at the table

186

under the vines and drank it in sips. He looked grey and tired. He was old, I saw. Old age was coming to him as even greater thinness, a stringiness, a revelation of bones and sinews. It was the gift of his class that he could make it look like a form of beauty.

It's been a long day, he said.

Jeannie brought him to his room. She took charge of him. They went into the house, into the silence. I heard no more.

Bill and I were the strangers, we were the only ones who had never been here before even though it was probably our honeymoon in the city across the water that brought my father here in the first place. He always fed on other people's experience.

In the afternoon the air seemed to settle in my room, a viscous fluid slowly reducing in a hot pan so that the slightest stir left a visible wake. I slept and woke naked and covered in a slime of sweat, sore and slightly panicked, conscious of having passed a troubled hour or two but unable to remember anything other than the feeling of anxiety. In other circumstances I might have called it desire or fear. I took a cool shower. Afterwards the water dried on my skin. The silence of the big hot house. A feeling of fullness, secrecy, intensity, mourning. There were moments, instants really, when I thought someone was about to cry. It might have been me. I thought about Bill and the researcher going at it, the slime of sweat separating them, Bill's blubbery sex on her tiny frame. I thought about Jeannie knowing. Father's pity. Richard's amusement. Bill can't keep it in his trousers.

I saw that they were friends, Father, Jeannie, Richard Wood, and that somehow in the wreck of our times I had drifted out of the way and Jeannie had found a comfortable inhabited place. A nest. I was the odd one out. I fell asleep eventually and woke about four o'clock. Some of the brutal heat had gone.

There's no time like the present.

I heard snatches of conversation. Bill was back. He was with the camera crew in the garden setting up for the first interview. Sound, light, colour temperature. The shadow of the olives and the vines and the lemon grove. I heard him say that he was aiming for something biblical, a Caravaggio effect. He had no idea what he was talking about, of course, though it all seemed to be a common language. He could say it and they could make it happen. The terms, properly understood, made the world. The interview would be tomorrow, the morning of my father's birthday. Bill sometimes talked in terms of restoring my father's reputation, but he was talking about his own.

Richard and Jeannie were somewhere.

The geckos were still as stones. The cicadas called. There was no birdsong in the sun. There's no time like the present.

Across the way the old woman moved through the shade with her hoe and her can. There was a chair by the lemon tree and the ground looked like dust. There was a gecko on her wall, though you would think he was a stone unless you looked long at him. He was perched on the edge as though he were preparing to jump. Goodbye cruel world.

I doubt geckoes think much of the world. They have all the appearance of cynics.

A long time ago on the island I saw Jeannie climbing the watchtower wall. I thought she would fall. It must have been before Em died, because I imagined her falling straight down to the water, her perfect child's body, her fading call like a bird dipping below the cliff edge. And then another time she was sick, but I did not experience the same furious joy or disappointment; it was just a long wait, sitting by her bedside with my mother and Em, and Em was sleeping. All children have these fantasies of destruction and forsakenness. If anything in my training could help me it was the knowledge that families are complex mechanisms, like intricate inter-related clockworks without clocks or time.

In the early evening I swam to clear my head. I needed to shake the heat from my heart. I could hear the brassy racket of the cicadas. It might have been time ringing in my ears. I swam out further than the boats. Out to where I could feel the current of the Tyrrhenian sea sweep around the headland taking me south towards Africa. Out in the deep sea you take a larger view of things. Continents come to mind, rivers of ocean, rivers of wind. I saw the broken lines of the island, the old volcanic ridges. I saw that there was an islet at one end joined to the rest by a bridge. And at the other was a walled village. I remembered my father saying the name – Terramurata. I saw the fire and ash of a million years frozen in time, the island thrust from the earth, the great maw and the smoke and the bubbling stone. Out I went. I saw my father's house, high up on the spine of the island, and someone standing outside. Could he see me? I recognised his shape, and, now that I was looking from a distance and could see only the shape of him, I saw that he had developed a stoop. Did he pity me? Poor Grace is married to Bill who can't keep it in his trousers, he doesn't even make a secret of it anymore.

There's no time like the present.

I swam back.

Out of my world.

I wore my bikini and a fine muslin shirt. I was long and straight and fit still.

I sent Bill a text. It was the least I could do. Fair warning. I met him in the garden of the Hotel Riviera. There was bougainvillea and a few waxy petals of gardenia. That dense, almost unbreathable air they make. You could drown in the scent of gardenia. Somewhere above us in a hot little room the researcher was rearranging her face. Putting her make-up on. A little bitch. They were all little.

I told him there in the garden. It was over.

He put his back to the balustrade and folded his arms. I knew Bill. I had studied his moods for years. I sensed a crisis. Something had unblocked in him. I prepared myself.

He said nothing for a time. Then very calmly he said: You knew I'd be like him.

He took me by surprise. First I wondered who he meant. Then I wondered if he was right.

He said: I knew that was why you married me. From the beginning. What does your lot call it? The Oedipus Complex? Isn't there a cure for that yet? In fact can you cure anything at all?

He laughed loudly. It was an unsettling artificial sound.

But I'm the soul of discretion, he said. Don't think I'll mention it. To your fucked-up family. Or Richard. Richard would put it in a poem. Mum's the word.

I tried to match his calm.

I want a divorce.

And you're welcome to it.

That's it then.

What's all the fuss about? You could have said it anywhere. You could have sent me a fucking solicitor's letter.

There's no time like the present.

He pointed at me. Now I saw that his hand was shaking. Anger. Careful, Bill, anger will kill you. His father died of a stroke at fifty-seven. And now that I looked more closely at him I saw that he was sweating.

His breathing was shallow. Bill was afraid of me. I knew what would come next.

Look at you, he said, you're like a stick insect. You're sick. If you'd seen a doctor years ago we wouldn't be like this now. You're completely fucking mad. You probably thought I'll bring him out to this fucking shit-heap island complete with BBC fucking film crew and then I'll ruin his fucking film. Do you know how much setting this up cost? Do you have any idea what will happen to me if I don't pull it off? On second thoughts, of course you do. It was all part of your calculations wasn't it? This is your revenge.

You should see yourself, Bill. You're shaking like a leaf. I thought you'd take this like a man.

Fuck you. Your whole family is screwed up. You picked the right profession. You're the worst of them all. All these years I've put up with your nerves and your fucking obsessions and your moods. You'd like to drive me over the edge, wouldn't you Grace? Another suicide? Someone else to fall off a cliff?

And so on. It was a brutal affair but I knew what I was doing. We were wrestlers but I was the only one with my feet on the ground. I had the strength of endings, of finality, of decision.

That's it Bill, it's all over and done.

Then I said, Be on your best behaviour at the birthday party, Bill. I promise you a treat.

He stared at me.

What are you up to now?

All the next day I stayed away. I wandered the island roads as far as they would take me. Bill hadn't come home.

The late afternoon bus was the pleasure of bodies, of crowding into an already crowded space, of hanging from a strap and feeling myself pushed this way and that by the contrapuntal sway, the press of people; the pleasure of smiling, the chatter, the music of happening. There was a space beneath my skin that wanted compression, that felt the absence of another body. Ghostly figures of lovers and children, half-memory half-possibility; there was, at times, a fluttering that terrified me. I was thinking of severance and rupture and letting go. I was thinking of falling and jumping. I was thinking that this was the last time.

I felt emptied and filled by this crazy music, this cantata of community, of being together.

I felt I could face anything.

When I got home I found that Bill's clothes and laptop were gone. Where to? Wherever the little researcher was.

At my father's birthday dinner I sat with her. She had the body of a child and the eyes of a hungry dog. My father sat at the head of the table with Serena at his right hand and Jeannie at his left.

Bill was getting his film after all. Or calling my bluff.

He and the crew moved around the table, surveying us through the one good eye of the camera. When they came to me I waved. Hello Bill, lovely to see you. Mosquitoes swarmed in the glare of the lighting – Bill had been experimenting with his Caravaggio effect. Before we sat down to eat we had all been given our instructions and now our skin glistened with DEET. It's a hundred per cent effective, Bill said. He did not want the scene interrupted by people slapping insects or scratching. What he was hoping for, he said, was a Biblical solemnity and a twenty-first century joie de vivre. Even my father thought this was crap. Oh Bill, he said, you do talk the talk, don't you? He seemed relaxed. The paterfamilias, the successful man among his adoring family.

The dinner was catered by Hotel Riviera, my father told us. Everything we would eat was local. He made a little speech, standing at the head of the table, Serena gazing up at him. Even the wine was from the next island where the *biancolella* vines grew, an ancient local stock, a wine that had to be enjoyed while young. I tipped my glass to Bill, touché, I said, we had it for our honeymoon. People around me smiled.

The people who did the cooking, my father said, are neighbours, islanders all.

We were to feel virtuous because of all this. Never mind that his royalties alone would have bought half the island. We were to feel we were making a contribution. That this humble repast would make a difference to the world we had abused. In his heyday he was good at this. You were excoriated and affirmed at the same time.

We had fried flowers and little fish and mussels marinated in lemon and little parcels of cheese. Then we had a risotto bianco. Then we had chicken. The food was superb. No one can do a banquet like the Italians.

Anyone who had walked down through the grapes and the lemon trees might have met these fellows, he said, indicating the chicken and olive *secondi*. They lived in this very garden until their death and a very good time they had of it too.

He took pleasure in the reactions of the camera crew, their protests. We can't eat them now! But they did.

Bottles of young wine went round and round and afterwards there was grappa and Amaro Averna and Fernet-Branca. People took photographs. It was one of those perfect evenings. Father talked in a contrived way about the intensity of small, how the world needed it, how thinking big meant thinking energy, how rapacious capitalism had done for the world. He talked about Marx and Adam Smith and about low-energy, high-intensity production. About the greed of the corporation making water, earth and air into commodities to be exploited. About power and discourse and multitude. I recognised the language and ideas from writers I was reading myself. I was surprised that in all this time he had been thinking and reading, but there was also regret – that it was all too late, that he thought he had made his mark and it was the wrong mark. Or that time had erased it.

Once, he said, we thought we could invent a new politics, but of course, the old problems were still there and they had their politics too.

It was the lesson or the gospel or whatever it is they read. The dead air of a church service had settled on us. If there had been incense I would not have been surprised. All these solemn men. I wanted to say that feminism had done more to change the world than anything they could imagine. But there were other things I had to say.

His next lesson was, We missed our revolution.

First I almost laughed aloud, then I coughed loudly, the sound ending in a splutter. It may have been a bit theatrical, but I was conscious of the cameras. I heard Bill swearing somewhere outside the rim of light. I stood up.

I said I would like to take the opportunity to tell them that Bill and I were to be divorced. It might seem strange to say it here, I said, but since we were all gathered here together, breaking bread as it were, all the people concerned – I raised my wine glass first to the shadows where Bill was recording the moment, then to the researcher, then to my father – I was happy to be able to tell everyone at the same time. And to have it recorded for posterity.

My father said congratulations with as much irony as he could muster considering I had shattered the air of solemnity with this trivial revelation. But I saw him glance at the little researcher.

Serena had to have the divorce business translated before she would believe I could say it here in public. I waited. It sounded sweeter and truer in Italian. It sounded like poetry. Then she cried. She may have been one of those people who believed in marriage despite the evidence, despite being an installation artist from the left-wing city of Genoa, where, possibly, installation artists are regarded as real artists and not funny architects. Richard Wood watched me obliquely, tilted back in his seat, turning and turning the grappa glass between two fingers. Then I proposed a toast for my father's birthday. I wished him long life and happiness in his island paradise. The glass I raised was half full of the blackness of Fernet. Everyone blithely echoed my words. Irony glistening like broken crystal in the soft night. Then I recited a poem for him, or at least a stanza and a line. It was Sylvia Plath:

> *So I never could tell where you*
> *Put your foot, your root,*
> *I never could talk to you.*
> *The tongue stuck in my jaw.*
> *It stuck in a barb wire snare.*

They didn't do toasts like that in the BBC.

My father stared at me. Serena wanted a translation. He put out his hand to her, but it was a gesture of control. She stopped.

I held my glass towards him again. I was conscious of the film moving frame by frame past the lens. I guessed that Bill would want this piece of drama preserved whatever about the divorce announcement. It would make riveting television, a reality show that was real. We're using film stock, he said, for that special atmosphere. You can't catch it any other way. Bill's old-fashioned virtues.

I'll say this, he made some pretty documentaries.

You are a guest at my table, my father said.

He pointed at me. He tried to say something else, the words stuttering like an engine gone wrong. I never heard what they were. Serena had her hand on his arm. A comfort or a restraint? What do you say now Daddy? What do you say now? He shook her hand off. Serena looked up at him. She was frightened. Some of us held glass, some did not, according to our place in the ancient pledge.

I may have been a little drunk. In my small frame even a little alcohol is enough.

Stop it, Jeannie shouted. She plucked at my clothes.

Lights camera action, I said. I may have waved my glass. Something gleamed in the light that might have been glass or liquid. This is better than Caravaggio, Bill, I said, The Death of The Family Newman, Bestseller's daughter fucks up the party. The one per cent warming party.

Christ, my father said, the film, for Christ's sake Bill, stop it.

I had his attention now. For the first time in my life.

But Bill said nothing. Good old Bill. The consummate professional. This is my parting gift to you Bill.

You kept it all under wraps, I said to my father, you buttoned us down, you were the master of ceremonies. You used us, you stole our island. You used our lives to make money. You're a charlatan. Here's to you, the great liar, the denier, the hider, here's to the redistribution of guilt to each according to his need. You made me

198

lie and swear to it. You wrecked my mother's mind. All these years I thought I was the one. All these years. Years and years of guilt. You ruined our lives. You could have saved her, but you didn't. If you loved her she would never have died. And Em would never have died. She'd be here at this table now drinking to your health, Emily my sister.

Some obstacle in my throat rising and falling like a cork on a wave. I was crying. I needed to master it. I took a deep breath.

Here's what I want to tell you, Tom, on your seventieth birthday: I blame you. We all do.

I knew I was crying. I felt as if my brain was breaking down. Those words stuttered out of me. I was disintegrating. I was shaking myself apart.

There was no glasshouse, I said.

I think I shouted it. The silence was instant. Only two of us knew what it meant. Everyone else held their breath.

He looked at me for what seemed like a long time. I could see he was trying to remember. Then he looked away and looked back again. There was something blind in the second look.

It was you, he said. You stole the book.

Yes.

I thought it was Maggie. I thought she was jealous of Jane.

I thought you would.

Now he was looking down at his lap. His head was

199

trembling, an infinitely small but definite vibration. Old age has laid her hand upon me. Bill and his camera moved a little closer.

It would have been my best book, he said. A certain bestseller.

It was a parcel of lies.

He looked at me again and this time there was an appeal in it. I could do it now, at his weakest moment, destroy him as simply as breaking a bird's neck. I said nothing.

What did you do with it?

I put it in a bin at Waterloo.

Did you read it?

No. A few pages, no more.

God.

I knew what it was about, I said. I knew the ending.

His lips and the tip of his nose were white. His breathing was fast. He was sitting very straight.

You're a vicious little bitch, he said. A sinister little bitch. Jesus Christ.

He stood up awkwardly and stumbled and sat down again.

No more, Serena said, please, *basta*!

She put her arms around him but she was looking at me.

She was a delicate woman. Those ideal forms that Italy makes. Her dark eyebrows were charcoal lines on a face that was shaped for pity. Her lips full as cherries. Her perfect breasts. Her boy's hips. Everyone at the table was in love with her. When she admonished me I sat down.

Jeannie comforted her. She held her hand. No one held mine. No one looked at me. I let the evening go. Darkness got past the lights. It flooded the lemon trees and fireflies appeared.

Fifteen

Richard is still sleeping, upstairs in our room, in the slatted evening. I come down for a lemon to squeeze in a glass, to make a cool drink to wake him with. But Grace is in the garden. In the heat still as hard and dry as a wall. Nothing moves. The long shadow of the house is a margin as sharp as a pencil stroke.

She has been waiting for me, I see. And now she has decided to confide in me. I don't want to know.

You'd think someone with brains wouldn't let this happen to them, wouldn't you, she says as I walk towards her.

She's drinking coffee. Black coffee. She's not planning to sleep tonight.

I mean this is my profession. The elucidation of fucked-up-ness to the fucked-up one. And I know, even we don't offer cures. We're not bone-setters. Different kind of charlatan altogether here.

Grace…

I know the research, of course, so very well, the dissociative amnesia hypothesis, etc etc. Oh *The Journal of Traumatic Stress* – what a great name for a magazine. Better than *Hello*. Catchy. I know it all and I'm still completely fucked. Look at me. I'm a human wreck.

Why are you saying this Grace? What are you telling me?

She stares at me but I can't interpret her stare. I think about what I am going to say. I want her to know that all of us have been marked in the same way. I say: Grace you don't have to tell me anything if you don't want to. I know. I was there, don't forget. We're sisters. Our past belongs to the two of us.

I stretch and catch her hands which have turned themselves into a bone-knot in front of her but she opens them and evades my grasp.

You weren't there, she says. You think you were but you weren't.

What are you talking about?

When Em died. I was there. I saw it. I didn't do it.

It was an accident, we…

I was supposed to be looking after her. That's clear. You know how she could always get away.

She looked like a student enumerating a set of causes or effects. I almost expected her to count them on her fingers.

Em thought hiding was a game. Last year I treated a woman who believed she murdered her daughter. In effect she had because that was her world. In reality her daughter was alive and well and living in Canada.

She nodded slowly to me. As if she expected me to understand everything now.

That was how I remembered, she said. It happens like that. I remembered that I was over by the beacon, first Em was with me then she was gone. She was like a rat, she could just vanish. Then later I saw mother go up to the tower. I saw Em on the wall. That's how I knew where to find the body. After that it all made sense. But Jeannie, the thing is, it was my day.

I saw that her hand was trembling where she rested it on the table. But her gaze was steady and cold.

Go ask Richard, she said. He knows everything.

In sleep there's something childlike about all of us — the way he wets his lips and swallows, the way he keeps his hands in loose fists on his paunch. An old man's paunch or a child's. He was never old until now. The usual background noise of this manic island, full of brief faceless events, always happening elsewhere, not here in this noiseless bubble. I kneel beside him. The skin of his ears is so pale that it seems almost translucent.

Richard, I say, Richard, wake up. I want to ask you something.

What force can a thought or memory have to change anything? An immeasurable force, a billion times lighter than a cobweb. A realignment of neurons, no more. But a bomb too. Whole men passing at the time are maimed forever. Memory is a war.

Jeannie, I was dreaming.

Richard, tell me the truth about what happened.

Christ, I'm not even awake, what are you after now?

Tell me about Em.

He sits up and rubs his eyes.

Oh God, he says, every time I wake up it seems to be worse. Some morning I'll wake up and it'll be dark.

What happened to Em?

He turns his face entirely towards me but he looks sideways at something else. I can't, he says, I can't. You know the story as well as I do. Why are you asking me?

I don't know the story. We knew nothing. We were children.

Tell me what you know, he says.

She fell off a cliff, Richard. She was playing a game with Grace. It was Grace's day. That's what we told the police and the coroner. She was playing some dangerous game and she fell off the wall. We all swore to it except mother and she was mad, anybody could see that.

He looks at me. His look is intense. Babies too have this blank intensity, but we know they see only light and dark.

He shakes his head. Ask Tom.

But I can't, not him. He's the last one I could ask.

He turns his face away again.

He says, That night, when your mother was raving – Tom and I – it was terrible, Jeannie, terrible. You children were crying uncontrollably. You probably don't remember that, but I'll never forget it. First your mother and then you two. She started you off. There was wailing all over the house. It was like something from a play. We could hardly think straight. We swore that night and I'm not going to break my oath. Not to you or anyone. Ask Tom.

What are you saying?

For a moment he seems to be glaring at the distance, at the past or the future, except that I know there is no distance, only the present.

He stands up. Stop asking me questions. It's not my responsibility. Ask Tom.

He walks away.

What does Tom know? I'm afraid. Because it means Tom knows.

Richard, I call after him, Richard I'm worried about Grace.

And then comes the night.

The waiters are clearing the food, their shirts the colour of foam on a rough sea, the cold seas of home where gales flay the Atlantic. They are unbending and deliberate, the kind of people who believe in their work, craftsmen of good digestion – where else in the world could waiters have such dignity? People are easing back in their chairs. The dinner has gone well, it seems to me. Bill's cameras and lights failed to rob the occasion of its actuality.

Then, as they clear the last plates from the table, she leans towards me and whispers, I'm going to ask him.

Not here Grace, I say, the film crew…

No time like the present, she says.

I see that she's drunk. She proposes a toast that nobody quite understands but we all respond appropriately. Sylvia Plath, Richard whispers.

Then one of those inexplicable moments of silence, a confluence of silences, that sometimes separates a before and after, and into this silence Grace says: An angel passed.

Everybody looks at her.

That's what we say, Grace says, an angel passed, it explains the sudden silence.

Oh, Bill's researcher says, I didn't know that. How lovely.

Then Grace leans forward to look at Tom at the head of the table.

You know who the angel was, Father? Guess.

Stop Grace, he says.

Well, she says, turning towards the camera man, it could be my mother or it could be my sister Em. It could be either one since they're both dead. What do you think, Richard? Em, I'd say. I don't think mother was anybody's angel, do you?

Richard says, Grace, this is a birthday party.

Serena covers her face with her hands. She has an instinct for dread. She sees it coming. Her hands too are small. Her fingernails are painted red; in the light ten drops of blood on her forehead. Tom put his arms around her. *Carissima, non preoccuparti…*

Grace erupts into laughter. She repeats it several times. A birthday party, a birthday party, oh my God.

That's a good one. Happy birthday dear Father, happy birthday to you.

Tom points down the table. But he says nothing. An old man, I see for the first time properly, in his age, pointing a crooked arthritic finger, quivering and powerless.

Richard says, For Christ's sake.

Grace stands now, and holds her wine glass up for a toast. She wavers a little as though a breeze has moved her. I'm getting a divorce, she says. I'm following in my father's footsteps because my father always likes to come first. It's all right, Bill knows about this.

Silence, the film crew looking from face to face, the researcher blushing deeply. Then Tom says, Congratulations.

A glassy anger has set in him. Now I see that he intends to wait it out. That in time she would stop and go away.

Long life and happiness, Grace says, and many happy returns.

The bizarre thing is that everyone lifts their glass and repeats the toast. Long life and happiness. All round the table, everyone except me.

Oh, she says, I'm glad Bill is here to record this moment. One happy family toasting the *paterfamilias* in his island paradise. Well here's to you, the liar, the denier, the hider.

She drinks her wine and puts the glass down on the table. It tips over onto its side.

Here's to my father who fucked us all up, she says.

Cos' 'ha detto, Serena says, what did she say?

Richard says, You're drunk, sit down and shut up.

Tom says: It's no use Richard, Grace must have her day, there's no silencing her.

I pluck at Grace's shirt again. What are you saying Grace?

All this time, Grace says, he let us think we killed her. He made us lie to the coroner's court. Ladies and gentlemen, my little sister fell off a cliff, it was a child's accident, they said. Grace killed Em – by mistake of course, children do these things, they haven't reached the age of reason, can't be held responsible – all that. Grace and Em were playing their games in the watchtower and Em slipped, something went wrong. It was Grace's fault because it was Grace's day. Poor Grace, she'll get over it. But Grace never got over it, ladies and gentlemen. You know how it goes – Grace buried the truth in her body. Look at me. I'm a fucking stick insect. That's so predictable it's almost boring. So nineteenth century. Come back Sigmund Freud, where are you now when we need you? But forgetting was better than believing what I saw with my own eyes. Children do that all the time.

What are you talking about?

I saw her going up to the tower, Jeannie. She was calling for Em. She was really angry. She saw Em on the wall. I was watching. She was shouting. She climbed onto the wall but Em was up beyond the window. Do

209

you remember the window? That was always the test. Who would go beyond it? Well, it was Em.

It's not true, I say.

We heard everything in that house Jeannie, fucking and shouting and fighting and raving and lying. I heard them working out their story. It didn't matter what mother said because anyone could see she'd lost her mind with grief. No one would believe a word out of her mouth. Guilt, they would say, a terrible thing, poor woman, she should have taken better care of them, living on an island like that was mad, a crazy hippy thing. They planned what to say to the police and what to say to the coroner.

It's a lie, Tom shouts. None of it is true. Not a word.

Grace says, Mother caught her leg. She reached out and caught her leg and for a split second she had her. Then she was gone. You decided, she pointed her finger at Tom, you decided that could never be told.

I turn to Richard. Is it true? What Grace is saying?

He looks away. The silence lengthens but no angel passes. People are holding their breath. I am conscious of a tiny red LED on the camera to my left.

Richard shrugs.

We were afraid they'd be hostile, he said, like Grace says, the hippy woman, the wild kids. We thought they might even bring charges.

You bastard, I say.

I hit him on the shoulder once, twice. You bastard Richard.

Suddenly he leans across the table, leaning towards Grace.

I should have left you in the water, he says, you were always a dangerous bitch, I should have sailed away.

Too late, she says, you let your prick rule, you should have kept it in your trousers, your prick was your heart.

I never touched you.

Oh you touched me all right, but not the way you think.

Serena looks betrayed, wounded, angry. She is staring at Tom.

You made it worse for my mother, Grace tells Richard. Now she had to betray all her children. To keep your secret. And she did. Even in London all those years later she was still carrying your secret for you like a little cancer in her belly.

Tom gets up. He stands for a moment with his palms flat on the table steadying himself, I think he may say something, then he turns and walks up to the house. But on the steps he turns again. He pauses for a moment, collecting himself. I see a shiver pass through him like the first touch of wind in the leaves. Then he walks away.

I heard the researcher say, Can anybody tell me where the gate is? Serena sat down beside me. She touched my face with the back of her hand. *Ti voglio bene*, she said. What does it mean? Love, it must mean. How much did she understand? She put her arms around me. I looked for Grace but she was gone. I was shaking,

211

a physical rigor that started in my feet and ended in my face. I thought I would shake myself to pieces. I was crying. Serena murmured her soft affections and I was thinking of Jane's room in Kingsland with its coloured wineglasses and mirrors and her little glass seal. And outside the crazy logic of Kingsland High Street with its hucksters and its Turkish social clubs and its long-faced carpet shops and police cars screaming by to the murders of Hackney.

A man said to me once – he was a fellow of Wadham College, a poet and friend of Richard's: There are only three important questions and upon a true understanding of their answers depends happiness. What are things really like? What should our attitude be towards them? What will we gain from this attitude? The answers? He produced the three words slowly, like a magician producing a surprising object right under my eyes: Unknowable; Noncommittal; Serenity. Others laughed. It was at a party, academics all, mostly scientists of one kind or another, a group standing in a loose circle holding G&T, wine, beer, listening, waiting for the punchline they did not understand. But this man was in deadly earnest and I was caught off guard by his ferocity, trying to sort the questions and answers. It felt like one of those exercises children are required to do, joining objects that belong together with criss-crossing lines: apple with tree, cow with milk, dog with bone.

What are things really like? Unknowable.

What should our attitude be towards them? Noncommittal.

What will we gain from this attitude? Serenity.

It came back to me as the first grey light began to select objects – my pillow, my bedside light, the frame of the bed, Richard's blank face. I had been awake all night, turning the past in my hands like a glass ball, one of those glass mooring buoys that used to wash up occasionally after a winter gale long long ago. Before sleep we had the following brief exchange: All my life I thought it was Grace. It wasn't Grace. Where is Em? Em is buried in Tiraneering churchyard, beside Flanagan the farting cat, I rescued him from a career of butchering baby rabbits, I'll take you to see her grave. Why didn't you tell me before? We swore. How many fucking times did you swear anyway? Just once, he said, but it covered everything.

Sixteen

Bill didn't come home. I wasn't surprised. I heard he was living with someone in Putney. I heard she worked in a fashion magazine. His next real manifestation was a Form D10: the petitioner therefore prays that the said marriage may be dissolved, etc., etc. He cited unreasonable behaviour as the grounds for divorce; it seemed a bizarre choice to me, but my solicitor assured me it would make no difference. I went out to dinner to celebrate, but afterwards, coming home on the busy bus, I felt my life had somehow darkened, that a shade had fallen or perhaps a filter that eliminated certain characteristics of the light. For a long time there was something tenebrous even about morning, and nights were bleak. We are to think that the departure of someone who has been part of our psyche, no matter what role they played, must inevitably be felt as loss, and I suppose I was bereft in some way, even if at the conscious level I was happy to be rid of him. Anyway, I survived. I had lunch with Jeannie near her college. She told me that Richard was staying for a while, would I like to come round for dinner, he'd enjoy the company and talk of old times. I saw what she was doing. But I didn't need another father in my life. My first experience was a bad one. I told her he was taking advantage, that he was using her, that they had used all of us. He's frail, she said, he's going blind. Not too blind to bloody go to New York. Oh, she said, they looked after him there.

One winter's night I got a call from Jeannie. He's dead, she said, he died peacefully in his sleep, heart failure, his ashes are to be scattered on the island, will you come?

I snorted. Heart failure.

Well, will you or won't you? Serena phoned me. She was distracted. She was crying on the phone. She's never been to Ireland. You speak fluent Italian, you could make it easier for her.

I'll have to think about it. You heard what he said; he said I wasn't his child. He told me once that he only had two children, but I didn't understand. Whose child was I then? Richard's? That'd be a turn up for the books.

Oh Grace, he didn't mean it, he was so upset that night. He would have said anything to hurt you.

I saw that Jeannie thought of it as a metaphor, a form of rejection not a statement of fact. She thought I *was* his daughter but he wanted me not to be. Whereas I thought I was Richard's, I probably always knew it, and Jeannie was bedding him, and the truth would be unbearable to her. Oh this rage for conclusions. I wanted to tell her, just to be rid of it, to finish, but I held my peace. She *was* my sister, no matter what.

He's dead now, she said, it's over, it's just a funeral, we can do that for him.

I remembered attending the funeral of a patient who had committed suicide. He was buried, I remember, in a place called Woodlands of Remembrance, every kind of deciduous tree that grew in Britain, the advertising said, was represented there. I don't think the family went to the trouble of reading the literature. My patient had hanged himself from a sycamore tree in his garden.

I said: Better to stand in the middle of Dalston Junction and scatter him in the traffic. He had a high old time there in the sixties and seventies.

But it's not just that, I said, it's the island too.

Her reply was almost a wail, a child's cry: But we're innocent!

Don't be ridiculous, I said, there's no such thing.

Oh for Christ's sake, not more of your bloody psychology. We didn't kill Em, that's what you said.

That's what I said.

I couldn't help it then, I never could. That bitter ice inside. The only thing that held me together was emptiness, what held my sides together, kept my mouth closed or open, pumped my blood. Look at me – I never had breasts, for years I never menstruated, I has half-woman, half child, a hybrid, a monster, a not-child, not-woman, not-wife, not-mother, not-lover. A listener, if there is

216

such a species, I lived in the voiceless underwater of guilt. There was never a world where I was myself, and therefore I never was. Long ago I realised that I hated myself more than any of them.

I found myself sitting at my kitchen table moving things about: a book, a salt cellar, a knife. My mind was crowded. I could hear my heart. How long had I been sitting here? I was suddenly terrified of the darkness outside. I got up and drew the blinds. Then I felt closed-in. I opened them again. I sat down again. I moved things on the table. Again.

We scattered his ashes on the island. It was his will. The day was blustery. A cold wind from Greenland or somewhere else to the north west had cleared the air. There were occasional heavy showers and strong gales, but you could see forever. The rocks were as clean as monuments, their striae and strata marked out like the grain of old wood. Richard made the arrangements and we went out on a fishing boat. It was there waiting at the pier when we arrived, lifting and falling gently in the refracted swell from the harbour mouth. And while we waited we watched heavy seas breaking outside the harbour. Richard and Jeannie came in his car. Serena and I hired one. It was her first time in Ireland. Everything was so neat and organised, she said, the fields were clean, the houses were clean and big too. Were they the houses of rich people? What did it cost to buy a house in Ireland? Did people own their own farms? She was excited, she said, to see Tom's fatherland. In Italian, fatherland is feminine – *la patria*. It seems somehow less threatening, less brutal, but it sent young men to war just the same and plenty of other savageries are done in its name.

Tom was on the back seat in a small wooden box of cedar; inside there would be a screw-cap plastic jar and the contents would be Tom. We come down to so little. The shakings of a tea caddy, with stray fragments of bone. After the fire we are not even clay.

I pulled over on the hard shoulder as we came into the bay to give Serena a chance to see. The empty moorings, the trawlers riding at the pier, the grey bay was dark and speckled with white. I said: We were like fish, we spent so much time in the sea. I remembered that when Jeannie was small she couldn't pronounce the letter 's'. And so she used to ask me to go wimming. My father picked it up and for years he could make us all laugh by suggesting that we wim on fine evenings. The telling was difficult in my mixture of Italian and English and Serena had to be told more than once. And then she turned fully round in her seat and did that Italian thing. She stroked my cheek with the back of her and said, *Carissima, ti voglio bene*. It made me cry. She held my hand. Serena the comforter. But it was she who was bereft.

The trawler landed us at the pier under the old tower. Jeannie and I looked at the place where I found Em. We

218

caught each other's eye. Here in the lee of the island the water was the same translucent green and I could see the stones at the bottom and the sea's long hair, kelp and bladder-wrack, lying out in lines with the current. We made our way along the old road until the place where it had fallen into the sea and then we went up into the fields. I saw again the jurassic fronds of the bracken, the quivering webs. Seabirds called. The sea thundered onto the shore and the shore stood its ground and drove it back. But there were losses. With each wave something died.

The house was still dry. The roof had not fallen in. There was glass in the windows. The door was still locked. Richard, of course, had the key. We went inside. Serena went everywhere. She went upstairs and we heard her creaking about. There was some kindling by the fire. An ash block was a nest of woodlice. They had hollowed it out. Jeannie took it outside and shook them out. Then we burned it. The flame warmed us even though the room slowly filled with smoke. Nobody really spoke.

Richard had a hip flask and he cleaned four glasses with the tail of his shirt. It was whiskey.

Here's to Tom Newman, he said. He was my friend and your father, your husband Serena. We all knew a different man, and the public knew another. But whatever we can say about him, we can say that he loved this place, this beautiful lonesome rock, this little patch of land where he first set roots, where he endured tragedy and loss, but also beauty and constancy and nature.

Jeannie caught my eye. Her look said, Not a word. Suddenly, inexplicably, I was happy. I winked and she smiled back. I was thinking, Expect an elegy to appear in the *Times Literary Supplement* set on an uninhabited island off the coast of Ireland, waves, seabirds, stones, an old house, a small gathering toasting in Connemara whiskey. It smelled like Connemara. It had that smoky texture. And I was thinking, This is Richard, so full of shit and self-importance, but constant to himself and to us; for all his faults, I love him too. The thought was liberating. I raised my glass with the rest of them and drank it back. The taste of flame. Here's to you my father, my lost father, my past, my mother, my sister Em.

The night of my return I got a call from an Irish journalist who first of all said he was sorry for my trouble, that old Irish formula of communal sympathy. His accent comforted me, his consonants like boats thudding softly against each other in a still harbour. He had seen the obituary on the *Guardian* website, he said, it was a good one. It was signed by Richard Wood. For some time he had been trying to piece together the story of our tragic family. They were his words. He remembered seeing us coming and going when we were children, exotic outsiders, the children of a famous writer. He remembered the time my sister died. My mother was beautiful. I was moved when he said that. He had grown up on the mainland in sight of the island, he said. They all knew about us in the village. The fishermen and boatmen carried the news. He called us the hippy children. He wanted to interview me. He was working up an article but he thought he might write a biography of my father and my family.

We're nothing special, I told him, life is a play before mourners.

But I told him what I could. There was a film, I said, very Caravaggio, very biblical. It hasn't been broadcast. They were worried about it, apparently, but maybe now … He could contact my ex-husband about that. I gave him a number. Then I told him that nobody knows how families work or fail, especially not anyone in my profession. It's a net made of lies and power and we pick at this filament or that and think we have everything in our hands. I remember someone saying to me once that you never know what goes on inside someone else's door. It should be the motto on every psychologist's desk. I certainly know nothing, I said, I've never known anything. I've fucked up and fucked up and no lesson has ever penetrated my skull. I've lost everyone. Or almost everyone. Except for my sister.

Are you all right, he said. Would you like me to call someone for you?

He sounded shocked. I don't think he was taking notes.

Who could you possibly call, I said. This is the modern fiction, that there's always someone to talk to.

Sure you're upset at the minute, he said after a short pause, I'll call back another time. In a couple of weeks. I shouldn't have rung at all.

221

I hung up. I was finding it hard to breathe.

The phone rang again almost immediately. Will it ever stop? Heartbreak must be like this, something both definite and incomprehensible. I took it off the hook.

I went into the bedroom. I opened the bottom drawer of my dressing table. It didn't open easily. A Marks & Spencer's bag was blocking it. The olive green plastic had hardened in the darkness of the years. I took my father's book from it. I hadn't looked at it since that day in the train. The hottest summer on record. I put it on my bedside table, a solid block of typescript. Time had finished it. I knew the ending now.

Opening the drawer was like drawing a deep breath. I could begin again.

I could build something with that block. I sat down and opened my laptop. I started a new document. I typed my first words. I already knew what they would be. It was as if I had been composing them for years, but in truth they came to me on the island, that day after we had opened the twist-cap and offered his ashes to the wind and the stony beach. It was sheltered there and though the sea ran rough and hard and cold outside, the small waves made no sound we could hear. He blew away onto the tide and we put the heavier parts into the heather at the field's edge. I remembered the seagull's bones. If I could have prayed I would have, but my mother neglected to teach us about eternity.

A long time ago I had two sisters and we lived on an island. There was me and Jeannie and Em. Our house had

two doors, one to the south, one to the north. Its garden looked
towards the setting sun.

I would write it for Em, for the life she never knew, the loves she never found, her undreamt of children.

The moon over the city. The rag-tag roofs of east London, its merry gables and hips and saws and skillions and mansards and pavilions. Far below an ambulance was trying to edge between two badly parked cars. Its lights were winding silently. Down the street a red man changed to a green one but no one was there to make the crossing. There were pools on the road. There is a game for every eventuality. Tomorrow is a spinning coin, heads or tails, nobody knows which is better. I turned the radio on. It was the shipping forecast. They were giving Lundy, Fastnet, south-westerly six to gale eight, occasionally severe gale nine at first. I don't know why it made me cry. I thought of the wind driving over the island and children sheltering in their beds, darkness hammering on the roof. Life blows through like a hurricane stripping everything from us, leaves from a tree, old washing from a clothesline, illusions, dreams, affections, hope. The wind in the walls said, Lonesome child go away, go home, childhood is a shadow on the floor. I turned but my mother was not there. I saw a crow breaking a mussel on a stone. He had the shell trapped under his claw. Water rushed in and out, sweeping the ground from under me, drawing me on a long cable, its windlass far away.